The Red Z

DIANE M. MITCHEL

Print ISBN: 978-1-66786-622-2
eBook ISBN: 978-1-66786-623-9

For my Busia Emily

THE INSPIRATION

When the phone rang, I recognized a Washington State area code on caller ID. My first thought, "Who died?" As I cautiously whispered a "hello?" the voice on the other end was that of my uncle, Henry, better known as Chip. We rarely spoke to each other via telephone, but communicated a few times a year through greeting cards and notes, mostly addressed to my mother.

Luckily no one had died, but Chip said he had a big favor to ask; could I possibly bring my mother, his sister, from Ohio to Washington to help celebrate his 80th birthday? His children were giving him a big party, and he wanted his favorite little sister there. I told him I would absolutely love to comply, but would have to do some careful thinking and planning. My mother had been living with us for about three years at this point, and was in the throes of Alzheimer's disease. Although she was mobile, and otherwise healthy, the bastardly disorder had robbed much of her short term memory, often rendering her incontinent as well. Most of the day she followed me like a puppy, although if I were pre occupied with a task, she would wander. She could disappear in an instant at the market, and show up meandering in the parking lot with items she collected, usually a chocolate bar and a trashy tabloid. I often wondered how we didn't get arrested. This was not going to be an easy trip.

Another one of my cousins was also going to fly to the celebration from Wisconsin with her 87 year old dad. Uncle Lawrence however, was in great shape, physically and mentally for his age, and was very excited to reunite with his last two surviving siblings. How could I not go? Besides, my cousin said she and Lawrence would be there to help. We would rendezvous in Chicago and all fly out from there.

The short flight to Chicago went well. Mother was very compliant, and followed wherever I went. Still having a great sweet tooth, snacks were plentiful in my carry on. I dreaded the long flight to Seattle, and then the ferry ride to Chip's house, but I had my Uncle and cousin for moral support. Unfortunately, the flight to Seattle was forced to land in Boise because of weather, and the next open flight out to Seattle was the next morning. The Airline gave us vouchers for nearby hotel rooms, and meals. Mother was in a tailspin. Nothing was familiar to her. Explanations were futile. In the days before cell phones, I had to contact Chip and relay the new plans. By the time we finally settled in the hotel, we were all exhausted, and mom fell quickly asleep. When I told one of my other cousins I was taking mom on this "adventure", she sent me a small package and told me to pack it in my carry on (pre 911!). It said "open in case of emergency". I came across it getting my toiletries out of my bag. This was "an emergency". To my delight, it was a mini bottle of *Southern Comfort* whiskey. I think I drank it in one long gulp. God Bless her!

The next thing I remember is waking to go to the bathroom and finding mom's bed empty. The hotel room door was open. I bolted out of bed to find mom wandering the halls in her nightgown. Finally getting her settled back down, I awoke a few minutes later to find her throwing things out of my suitcase looking for underwear so she could get dressed. And so our little game continued in the early hours. By the time we were ready to leave the hotel to catch our flight, I was mentally and physically exhausted, and we had a lot of travelling yet ahead to us. Sweet rolls and lots of coffee helped us both. Uncle Lawrence, and Cousin Anita were no worse for the wear, and enjoyed their mini-vacation and meals at the hotel.

The rest of the journey is a bit of a blur, but the weather cooperated, the scenery was breathtaking, and mother was able to converse a bit with her brother Lawrence at the airport and on the ferry. She may not have known where she was, but she definitely knew him. The reunion of the three siblings as we left the ferry was a sight to behold. Tears of joy (mixed with exhaustion) fell like rain all around. Anita and I knew we did the right thing, making this journey.

The three hour time difference took its toll. Mother was ready for bed right after dinner, and awoke at 3 AM. She had completely wet the bed and was very upset. I did my best to quiet and calm her while not waking up the rest of the household. Nothing was familiar to her except my face. I got us cleaned up and to the kitchen where I rummaged for coffee and something sweet. Luckily Chip's wife was a baker extraordinaire, and mom was content with the luscious coffeecake. After that first night, things improved a bit. Chip took us sightseeing, and treated us to a lovely crab dinner. The next day, his children threw him a wonderful party, with lots of friends and neighbors, and mom seemed quiet, but happy.

The last day of our visit, we all pitched in and made a buffet from all the leftovers from the birthday celebration. Mom seemed so happy with her two brothers near. Everyone seemed to want to retire early as we had to leave to catch the ferry back to Seattle shortly after dawn. Chip and I were the last ones up. I saw what appeared to be tears in his eyes. He reached under a cabinet in the dining room, and said, "As I remember, this was your favorite". It was a bottle of *Jack Daniels*. I have no idea how long we sat there drinking, talking and crying. What I do remember, are the stories that came pouring forth from that gentleman, like they'd been bottled under pressure for years.

When we finally arrived back in Ohio, I headed for the nearest restroom, mom in tow, and burst into tears; literally uncontrollable sobbing. Strangers asked me if I was OK. I couldn't even compose myself to answer.

Poor mother was so confused. I guess I cried for the past I now knew, the overwhelming stress of the present, and for what I knew lie ahead. When I finally composed myself, I took my lovely sweet mother by the hand, and resolved not to let these stories be forgotten.

THE BEGINNING

Supposedly the climate of Wisconsin, especially central Wisconsin, is similar to that of Poland. Maybe that's why so many Polish immigrants settled there. It was probably easier to grow customary crops with familiar soil and seasonal changes. The flat prairies favored farming, and soft rolling hills and forests housed wild game. A myriad of lakes held multitudes of trout and blue gill. Adequate rain and moderate to severe winters were normal.

It was good to have Stan already in the States. He had written about the land he had purchased in Stevens Crossing. It was a large parcel, enough to certainly sustain them all. Stan even sent a few dollars to help pay the passage fee for his brother Jan and his family from Rotterdam to New York. The political climate in Poland had never been good and with tensions rising between occupying Germany to the West, and Russia to the East, and Austria-Hungary to the south, many Poles were leaving their homeland and all they had, for the unknown. Having Stan in Wisconsin was certainly going to make the transition easier. Stan's letters sounded so positive. Perhaps the United States would be their Promised Land. The farm in Stevens Crossing was already turning a profit, especially from the milk produced, and Stan had even found a neighbor girl, also an immigrant from Suwalki, to take as his bride. Their two young sons were American citizens. There was every reason to be hopeful.

Jan knew this would be most difficult on his young bride. His first wife, Viola, died tragically of pneumonia after less than seven years of marriage. Jan was only thirty, heartbroken, and widowed with a four year old daughter,

Josefa. He was estranged from his own parents because as staunch Catholics, they refused to accept his union with Viola, who was of Jewish descent. His only brother, Stan had left Suwalki to find his fortune in America. Their neighbors, the Ulewicz, helped with *Josie's* care, and treated her as one of their own. Emilia Ulewicz, their oldest daughter, was sixteen. She had a particular fondness for Josie that touched Jan. He could not help but be struck by her youthful beauty, as well. Her silky auburn hair hung halfway down her back visible under her babushka. Because she was unmarried, it was rarely worn braded or in a bun. Although formally uneducated, she was an intelligent girl, pious, and handy with the needle. Most in town thought she might enter the local novitiate. On Christmas day, 1898, Jan asked Mr. Ulewicz for Emilia's hand. His child bride and his child moved into Jan Zalewski's home and began a family of their own. First came Boleslaw (Benjamin), the first of his five sons, and daughters Bronislawa (Bernice) and Helena (Helen).

Emilia was barely twenty-five, with a step-daughter and three smaller children of her own. Jan was asking her to leave her home, her parents, siblings, church and homeland, and travel over 4000 miles to some foreign land. It would be no easy journey to be sure. They had to travel steerage class in order to conserve funds needed to get from New York to Stan's farm in Wisconsin. Josie and Ben would be alright she thought, but Bernice and Helen were just five and four, too young to understand why everything they knew was being taken away from them. Jan was a good man, but hard-headed. There was no talking him out of immigration. Stan's letters were added fuel, as were the constant rumors of War in Europe. And so like most women of her generation, Emilia kept her vow of obedience to her husband, and prepared her family for immigration to a new world.

The first leg of their journey was by rail from Suwalki to Warsaw, changing trains in Berlin to Rotterdam. The children, having never been on a train, thought this a great adventure. Emilia had never been out of their Polish village, so the excitement of seeing new places through the train windows temporarily masked her fears. When they reached Rotterdam, the reality of what they were about to undertake set in. Just communicating with the Dutch was problematic, trying to find food, toilets, and directions to the harbor. They were treated less-than-politely because of their common appearance and accents. Emilia began to feel like they were cattle being herded and prodded this way and that, and following blindly for fear of being lost in the shuffle of bodies and belongings. What were they doing? She prayed fervently to the Black Madonna, patroness of her homeland, that Stan's letters were true, and that America would be the haven they hoped for.

Elegantly dressed men and women traveling First Class caused the children to stare in awe. Ben seemed especially impressed with their finery and lavish possessions. Jan told him that perhaps these things awaited them, too, in America. That dream excited Ben and seemed to sustain him throughout the journey. The girls, having always seen Polish babushkas on women and never hats, laughed uproariously at the huge, feathered monstrosities worn by the elite, complete with umbrellas even when it wasn't raining, and gloves when it wasn't even cold! "Is this how they would have to dress in Wisconsin?" they asked.

She was prepared for the damp chill of steerage and even the cramped quarters, but not for the stench. Emilia was nauseated from the first day of the crossing. Because they were lowest class, they had to prepare their own meals and do their own laundry as best they could given the conditions. Her heart went out to those with infants in diapers, the constant chore of changing and washing, and of course, and the excrement contributing to the ever-present stench. Fresh air was not to be found in steerage. The Dutch steamship Noordam carried 1800 third class passengers this crossing.

Luckily, the children, either out of excitement or fear, were complacent. Ben amazed some of the other children, not to mention their elders, with his ability to whittle. His babka Ulewicz had given him a pocket knife as a parting gift for the journey, and Ben found he possessed a talent for carving the most incredible little figurines out of scraps of wood found round the ship. Emilia tried to entertain her daughters with stories and folk songs. She taught them elementary needlework, too, although the lack of light and air made her seasick doing so. Luckily there were other Polish immigrants aboard, so there were playmates for the children and confidants for the adults. A few knew rudimentary English, and they passed on their knowledge to Ben and Emelia; "Hello", "Goodbye", "Where is…" A strange language, so foreign sounding.

Jan was worried about his wife. She was so seasick she could not keep much food down. He had taken over much of the meal preparation, as this, too, sickened her. Emelia looked so thin and pale. What had he done, making them leave all they knew and loved for the unknown? Was it worth the price? Thank God the children were well, and that Emelia had a few new friends to care for her and help with the children. He prayed she would be better by the time they got to New York. What if she were too ill to emigrate? Would they all be sent back to Poland? So many worries. Sleep came with difficulty. Most nights were awash with "why dids" and "what ifs". Then there was talk of war. Always war. Would Poland ever be an independent nation, divided as it now was, as if so many pieces of a pie, among its neighboring border countries? Would there be war in America, too? The men onboard spent much time discussing this.

After enduring fifteen days at sea, ship's gossip spread that they would this day arrive in New York, America! The weather was warm and clear. A perfect July day. Luckily for them all, the crossing had been relatively unaffected by weather, thus somewhat "smooth", but Emelia was still extremely seasick and spent much time curled up in her bunk. When word spread that land was in sight, the children grabbed her from her bed, and the five of them clamored topside where the throngs of passengers of all classes and ethnicities, stood body-to-body, craning their necks to catch the first glimpse of Lady Liberty and their new home. As the infamous Statue of Liberty came slowly into view, strangers became friends, language barriers were broken, those with musical instruments broke into song, and many began to cry. Such a flood of emotion swept through the immigrants. Jan and Ben hoisted the younger girls on their shoulders to help them see above the swarm. For an instant Emelia forgot her misery, and felt the contagious joy.

As the steamship pulled into New York harbor, the joy began to dissipate, and nervous thoughts took their place. Will Stan be there to meet them, and vouch for them? Would he bring the train fare to Wisconsin as he promised? How will they navigate a huge city like New York, especially not knowing the language? Would she pass the entrance physical? She looked as awful as she felt. The fresh sea air felt good against her skin. With a quick prayer of thanksgiving to the Madonna for a safe crossing, she rallied all her remaining strength. Hopefully, the worst was over. She joined the other passengers going below decks to gather their meager belongings, holding fast to the little ones lest they be lost among the eager new Americans.

Debarkation was, as expected, long and tedious. First and Second class passengers were given a quick legal and physical screening, and allowed to leave the ship in Manhattan. Steerage passengers were fitted with large tags; their passenger numbers written on them, then they were shepherded onto large ferry boats headed for the American immigration point at Ellis Island. The sight of Manhattan was something Jan and Emelia would never forget. Such an immense concrete jungle! How would they ever navigate it? After a short ferry boat ride they again disembarked at Ellis Island where they proceeded to what appeared to be a huge palace. A beautiful, imposing, several storied building, similar to one she had seen in Berlin. America must be wonderland, indeed. Inside, however, the atmosphere was less than regal. The large three story great hall, had rows and rows of metal gates to keep people in neat single file lines as they awaited their turn to be formally admitted to the United States. The noise in the great room was deafening. Over 1,000 exhausted, somewhat foul smelling people all speaking in nervous and varied dialects, babies crying, tired children whining, not one knowing quite what to expect. It was foreboding.

After being checked against their ship's manifest number, they were ready for their medical examinations. Many Doctors were present who checked their face, teeth, ears, hair, and neck. Their eyelids were especially scrutinized for signs of the highly contagious and incurable "pinkeye". Stethoscopes listened to their hearts.

Luckily there were interpreters present, so when the Doctor questioned Emilia's thin face and "greenish" complexion, she was able to explain the horrific seasickness. She was allowed to move on. Past the first two hurdles. They were then asked to scale the two huge flights of stone stairs to the third floor. As Emilia looked up, afraid in her weakened condition she could not make the climb, she saw many faces looking down, observing the emigres as they journeyed toward the top. These, she later learned, were Doctors observing any physical or mental weakness that might be present. Six steps from the top, Emilia fainted.

She awoke in a cot with her family around her. When she realized what had happened, she burst into tears fearing they would now be sent back to Poland for her weakness! They family was told, via interpreter, they would have to spend the night in the third floor dormitory…rows of cots as far as the eye could see. At least it was clean, the air was not foul and the floor was not moving. They were given water, fruit juice and a hot meal. Helen slept next to her mother, the others each had their own cot. Jan was glad Emilia had their meager savings pinned to her undershirt. No telling who to trust now. He slept very little, his mind racing. What would tomorrow bring, would Stan know to wait? On the other hand, Emilia slept soundly, having re-hydrated, and able to keep some food down, exhaustion took over, and when officials woke her the next morning, she felt renewed. Jan, on the other hand, looked tired and worried. Having been convinced by her appearance that her "illness" was just a bad case of seasickness, the little family was allowed to finish their immigration process. They were then each asked to repeat their full name, and ushered to the money exchange where they could trade their Polish currency for US dollars. Jan, still dubious, hoped they were not being duped. From there they were taken to purchase rail tickets to their final destination. Because Stan was bringing money for this, they hoped against hope he was still waiting for them in the relative/ sponsor's area of the building.

Never in their lives had anyone been so glad to see anyone than Jan and Emilia were to see Stan! There he was, hat in hand, just as they had remembered him in Poland; perhaps a little older and perhaps a few pounds heavier, but he looked well and prosperous. Josie and Ben had been small when their Uncle left for America, and so they were re-introduced to him and to the girls. After a quick chat, and a few happy tears, they boarded the ferry for Manhattan. Uncle Stan treated them to an American "Hot Dog". The children and their parents had to be assured that Americans did not really eat dogs! The new sights of America were never-ending; trolley cars, automobiles, tall, impressive buildings; "skyscrapers" they called them! An impressive horse drawn carriage took them to another palatial look-ing structure. Ben asked if the "King of America" lived here. Uncle Stan explained that, " America has no king, but instead a President, and his name was Theodore Roosevelt. Furthermore, he lives in Washington, D.C., about 200 miles from here. Maybe we will be lucky enough to visit there someday. This was not a palace at all, but the train terminal. It is called Grand Central Station." This was like no train station they had seen, not even in Berlin. It was 6 stories high, covered one entire square block and was decorated with a dome like structure at each of the four corners, and above each of the four entrances. No wonder they called it Grand. The poor baby girls were not impressed having fallen asleep in the carriage. Stan carried the bags, and Jan carried Bernice. Ben carried Helen. Emilia carried what she could while trying to answer all Josie's questions about the miraculous images she was seeing.

When Uncle Stan returned from the ticket kiosk inside the sparkling, new Grand Central Station, he wore a forlorn expression. It had been several years since he had made this journey himself, and did not realize the children each had to pay full price for a ticket. He had made the assumption, the two youngest could ride free. This was not the case. He was several dollars short. Jan told Stan they had brought a little money with them, but Stan felt this would be needed to buy food for their journey, and the transportation from Chicago to the farm in Stevens Crossing. A fellow Polish immigrant, hearing their pitiful conversation, told Jan that he was headed to the Singer Sewing factory in New Jersey, where they were hiring. There was also a boarding house on premises, but only men were allowed to stay there. Perhaps Emilia and the children could go ahead with Stan, and Jan could work at the factory for a few months and save up for rail fare to the farm in Wisconsin. The decision was made hastily as the last train was leaving in thirty minutes for Chicago and their future. What if he could not get a job? Where would he stay; what would he do? He spoke no English. His fellow immigrant told Jan he could follow him to the Singer factory. He had directions on papers sent to him in Poland by relatives in New York. What choice did he have? He kissed Emilia and the children and thanked Stan for taking them to Wisconsin. Addresses were exchanged, and Jan promised to write every day, coming to them as soon as he were able. With fifty American cents from his brother in his pocket, The American reality began.

Ambrose Dubroski was young and single. He was engaged to a girl back home, and hoped to make enough American dollars to bring her over to New York where they could build a life together. Unlike Jan who was a farmer by trade, Ambrose was a mechanic. Although he had no formal schooling, he had a knack for being able to assemble and/or fix any type of machinery. Industrial America seemed to hold the key to his future. There was no farmland to be seen in the asphalt streets of New York. What would Jan possibly have to offer the Singer Company?

The two Poles made their way through the never-ending maze of streets, following Ambrose crude map. Jan was astounded by the sheer number of people! Everyone seemed to be in a hurry. The two walked for hours, stopping only to buy an apple to sustain them. They had to reach the factory before quitting time. The next leg of their journey involved taking a ferry boat across the Hudson River to New Jersey. A little more money for fare depleted. At least the ferry station offered restrooms and running water. After a short distance, they could view the outline of the huge sewing machine plant on the other side of the waterway. Once disembarked, they jumped on the back of a wagon headed toward the factory in the distance, and were thankful for the rest, and for finding their way through the concrete wilderness.

I. M. Singer could not produce his life-changing invention fast enough in Europe. Everyone wanted a Singer machine in their home. Therefore, he built a factory in the U.S. There was work assembling machines and building cabinets. The factory was a magnet for immigrants as it required quick and simple training, and little language skill. The wages were certainly more than he'd ever hope to make in Poland, even when they deducted for his meager room and board. They were both hired. Another hurdle overcome.

Jan made it his business to try to learn the new language as fast as he could, but there were so many foreigners often it was hard to tell who was actually speaking English. The work was not particularly difficult; in fact boring most of the time. He found himself picking up many new skills including sewing! He decided he would stay long enough to make money for his passage west, a few dollars to pay Stan for taking in his family, and to buy a Singer machine for Emilia. The Shop was hot in the summer, and freezing in the winter. Only the thought of seeing his little family again, kept him going. It was hard to resist the poker and dice games played after hours in the dormitory; he had no money to loose. He kept himself sane writing to Emilia each night and re-reading her letters from Wisconsin.

Emilia, Stan and the children made it safely to Chicago. Another impressive American city with so much activity! Stan told Emilia that there had been a terrible fire that burned much of the city, and that they were rebuilding, calling in the best and brightest new architects to make their city shine brighter than the one before.

Emilia was still not well. The train ride was better than the ship, but still the rocking motion made her ill. Luckily, the smaller children slept most of the time cuddled in their seats, eating some of the bread, cheese and apples purchased in New York for their journey. Ben, however seemed fascinated by everything and everyone he saw. When it wasn't too dark, he kept his face pressed to the glass window to view the passing countryside. He told his mother he was too excited to sleep. Perhaps he was a bit scared, too, as with Papa gone, he was now the responsible one.

They boarded yet another train headed north, with multiple stops in odd sounding places like Kenosha, Oshkosh and Milwaukee. Each seemed more "modern" than anything he had seen in Poland. The terrain, however, seemed much the same. Flat, fertile farmland, lakes, evergreens, and gentle rolling hills. It took a better part of a day to reach Stevens Crossing, and then another half hour by wagon to reach Uncle Stan's farm. As they passed a particularly flat and green parcel of land, Uncle Stan pointed out that this was to be Jan's land to farm and build his home. In the meantime, they would all stay with Uncle Stan and Aunt Genja.

Emilia was so exhausted and thankful to see another Polish woman, that she practically squeezed Aunt Genja to tears. How good to hear your native language, and be in a place that, although foreign, seemed familiar! The children gobbled the roast pork, fresh milk and potato pierogi. Even Emilia seemed to have gotten an appetite back. How she wished Jan were here to see this. She vowed not to be a burden to Stan and Genja, but to help in every way. The children would help, too, with some direction from their cousins. Ben said the first thing he was going to do was begin carving a wooden figurine to thank his Aunt and Uncle for taking them in; after chores, of course.

Emilia heard the rooster crow at dawn, but could not seem to fully awaken. It wasn't until little Helena was in bed shaking her, that she rose with a start. Where was she, what time is it, where is Jan? The children? Genja knew the poor girl was exhausted, so she let her sleep while she fed the children breakfast. Ben was already in the barn when she dressed and came downstairs. He was helping Uncle Stan and his cousin Mikel with the milking. Josie was helping mind the smaller children while Genja kept breakfast warm for the men. How wonderfully resilient children are. Weeks of travelling, hardships, heartbreaks, and they continue their routine as always. Emilia was glad school was not in session yet, so they could all help out on Stan's farm before Jan arrived. She asked Genja if her boys went to school. She said they both went until they were 10, and then were needed more at home to help manage the farm. Their daughter Anna, would probably follow suit. They could all read and write in English, but at home, Polish was spoken. Besides, the school was about three miles away.

The day was spent washing all their clothing. Emilia could still smell the stench of the steerage on her garments. It was a beautiful day, the freshly laundered items dried quickly in the warm breeze outside. Later in the day, the boys and the two older girls took turns bringing water from the pump to put on the stove to heat. Everyone was getting a bath. Usually, bathwater was shared by the children, but Emilia felt they were so filthy from their journey, that she gave all four their own tub full of freshwater. Genja's children all went off to the spring fed pond near the barn to bathe. This would become the custom for all of them for the rest of the summer. But for today, lots of soap and warm water. The soil and sweat of their journey could be washed away, but never the memory. Did Jan get the job?

Summer turned to fall. Autumn in Wisconsin was similar to autumn in Poland. Cool temperatures made for colorful, glorious foliage, also for lots of work, namely the harvest. Ben had proven to be a real help to Stan and his cousins, but every spare minute he had, he was whittling away at something. The figurine he carved for his aunt and uncle was a lovely pine swan. They were exuberant in their praise and put it in the center of their mantle. He was now working on something for their new farmhouse, to surprise Jan when he returned. Ben, and Anna were allowed to go to school. Luckily, Anna knew more English and could help Ben with his studies. They walked the three miles to and from school, until the snows came. If it was too deep, they were allowed to stay home. On rare occasions Uncle Stan took them in the horse and wagon if he had errands in town. Ben's English was improving. He was determined to learn, if nothing else, to stop the bullies at school from teasing him for the funny way he talked. He begged Emilia to speak English at home, but she refused, as this was Aunt Genja's home and her rules. Josie, at thirteen, was needed at home to help with the myriad of never ending chores. She was a decent cook, but was exemplary with a needle. Emilia had taught her to crochet on the boat trip over, and she excelled at it, making all manner of lovely things, as well as warm hats and mittens for the family.

Letters from Jan were always a treat, and saved for dessert, after their evening meal. He said he would miss them at Christmas, but promised to send a present for them all. Although he longed to be with them, he was making and saving some good dollars, and felt himself more productive in New York, than at the farm in winter. He sent his blessings to his brother and his family, and again his thanks for caring for Emilia and the children. Hurry Spring.

Their first Christmas in America. Stan, Ben and the cousins had had a successful farming season, and much luck with fishing and wild game. Therefore, Christmas Eve, would be the traditional meatless pre-holy day feast, with the customary twelve items on the table representing the twelve apostles. Smoked trout, mushroom pierogis, potato latkes, cranberry and strawberry jelly, freshly churned butter, warm yeast rolls, fried bluegill, bowls of cold beet zupa, kapusta with fried onions, plates of cheese, dried cherries and sweet and crunchy chruscki. It was glorious, if only Jan could be there! At Mass on Christmas Day, Emilia prayed to the Black Madonna, thanking her for delivering them safely to America, and asking her to protect her husband and to bring him back soon.

After a wonderful meal of roast venison and golabki, Uncle Stan announced he had a surprise. All the Children gathered around the fresh-cut Christmas tree. They had made all manner of homemade decorations including popcorn (which the new Americans had not seen before!) and cranberry garlands. Emilia went first. She asked Josie, as the oldest, to open the wrapped box which had been placed under the tree. After doing so, she carefully lifted out an angel. Emilia explained that she had asked Ben to carve its wooden head. She had then taken some of Josie's wool used for crochet to form "hair", and for the wings and dress, she used the fabric from the apron she wore during their crossing to the United States. This she embellished with the most beautiful embroidery. She asked Uncle Stan to put it atop the tree to always remind them of this year, 1907, when they came to America. Now it was Uncle Stan's turn. He left the room momentarily, and returned with a huge, heavy box which he scooted along the wood floor. It was post marked New York, New York, and addressed to Emilia Zalewski and family. Inside were sweet treats for each of the children and cousins, a cigar for Uncle Stan, a lace handkerchief for Aunt Genja, and a Singer Sewing machine for Emilia!

Jan couldn't believe his eyes. Each employee had received a Christmas card from their employer containing two dollars, even the Jews! Furthermore, they were treated to a better-than-average Christmas supper at the boarding house, complete with beer. The only thing that could make this day better would be being with Emilia and his rodzina. He hoped they received his surprise package. He was able to get an employee discount on the machine, and worked some overtime hours. He will have to stay in New York a bit longer, however. He glanced at the package that arrived for him last week. He knew it was for Christmas so he held out opening it until today. Inside, Josie had crocheted him a warm stocking cap and mittens, which he sorely needed for this cold New York winter, Ben had whittled a small replica of a buck that he said he shot with some help from Uncle Stan. How he had hoped to be there with his boy when he shot his first game. Next were cards and drawings from his two little ones, a jar of strawberry jam from Genja, and a sweet smelling letter from his Emilia saying his present this year would be coming at the end of January. Would he like it to be a boy, or a girl?

By Easter, Jan had saved enough to pay off the sewing machine and have money left for his passage to Wisconsin. To say he had lived frugally was an understatement. He was rail thin, and longed for some real Polish food. He must admit, however, that he had developed a taste for American "hot dogs", and sometimes treated himself to one. Not Kielbasa, but tasty especially topped with the pickled kapusta they called "sauerkraut". He almost wished he could stay and keep saving, but Stan had taken care of his family for nine long months, and now he needed to repay him by helping him get his crops in the ground. He was also so very anxious to see his family and meet his new son, who they decided to name after their savior, his brother Stan.

Ambrose had risen to the job of supervisor, his skill in mechanics becoming apparent. Jan would miss the young man. He was decent, smart and hard-working. They promised to keep in touch. The talented mechanic had sent for his fiancé, and she would be arriving in late April. Jan's English was still broken, but he had learned enough to get by.

This time at Grand Central Station in Manhattan, he felt a surge of confidence. He had a few dollars pinned to his undergarments, a rudimentary knowledge of the native tongue, and the deep desire to see his family, begin a new chapter in his life, and return to doing what he knew best. While waiting for the train to take him to Chicago, and ultimately to Emilia, he was drawn to the swarm of immigrants there. That feeling came flooding back; a cross between excitement and sheer panic, with a side of exhaustion. He could not help but pick up on an anxious conversation in Polish amongst the group. Jan felt a deep sense of pride when he could intervene and offer up some directions and advice. After all, he was now an American.

The trip to Chicago and beyond was relatively uneventful. Much of his time was given to daydreaming. A new son! He wondered if he'd look like Ben with a mop of dark, wavy hair, or more like Bernice with her light, curly mane. Jan was thankful to hear that Emilia had a reasonably easy birth, albeit on the coldest, snowiest day of the winter. The girls were captivated with the tiny infant. Ben was doing well in school he was told, and was learning to read and write some English thanks to his cousin's tutorials. Unfortunately, this may be the end of his schooling, as there would be much need of his services to get the new farmstead up and running. Jan sensed that his oldest son was a bit of a dreamer, or perhaps idealist. He had a definite talent for creating figurines out of wood, and seemed to be fascinated by the smallest things, like insects, for instance. Josie, he was told in Emilia's letters, was quiet, but a fine helper around the house and great with a needle. His heart swelled with pride for his wife and children, so brave for these last nine months.

Jan arrived in Stevens Crossing on a particularly cold and rainy Good Friday. It was hard to see much of anything of the scenery of Wisconsin because of the driving rain and foggy skies. Not even the ominous weather could dim his spirits, however, he was so excited to see his family. Stan met him with his wagon at the small train station. Grand Central it was not, but it was grand to him. On the cold, wet drive to the farm, Stan drove past the parcel of land that was to be Jan and Emilia's. Even in the rain Jan could see it was broad and flat, and had a perfect setting for a farmhouse near a stand of trees not too far from the road on which they were traveling. Stan halted the horse in front of what appeared to be a wooden pole with a sign attached; "J.

Zalewski" it said in bright red letters outlined in black. Underneath a large, red "Z", in the Polish tradition, had been hand carved. "Ben made this for you as a homecoming gift," Stan said. "The boy is very clever."

When they reached Stan's farmstead down the road, Jan was disheartened to know that no one was home. Being the good Catholic family, they were all in Church for Good Friday services. He could wait a few more hours, giving him time to get warm, and clean up from his journey. Stan left to get the family from St. Casimir's. As often seems to happen on Good Friday, the rain ended late afternoon, and by the time the family returned, the sun was peeking through the clouds. Jan had fallen asleep in front of the warm fire, and awoke as if in a dream to the children squealing, "Papa!" How delightful is was to hold Emilia in his arms again, and how overwhelming to hold his new son.

It was the most joyous Easter any of them will ever remember. The "resurrection" of their father from the agony of New York, and the rebirth of new life in the United States. His girls were resplendent in new dresses made by Emilia and Josie on the new Singer. His sister-in-law, Genja, made it her mission to "fatten him up", as she said he appeared too city pale and thin. After High Mass at St. Casimir's, Easter was a feast including traditional Polish dishes such as czarnina soup, succulent roasts of pork and duck, potato and cheese pierogi, kapusta with bacon, fresh spring grzyby (mushrooms) fried with onions, and hard boiled eggs. The eggs were almost too beautiful to eat. Emilia was very gifted at the art of pyzanka, or egg decorating using beeswax and a needle. The girls told Jan all about the process, and how they boiled the onion skins to make the rich amber dye. Ben and Josie had each made him an egg with *PAPA* written on it with the delicate wax. Jan hoped he would never forget the sensation of this day; the feelings of security, affection and tradition, mixed with anxious trepidation. Today the celebration, tomorrow the reality.

The following day, the brothers walked the land Stan had purchased for them; the parcels were side-by-each. Stan suggested they put their homes as close together as they could, and had already selected a place to put the home and barn. Jan agreed; not too far off the dirt road that passed his land, and with a stand of evergreens and hardwoods near for shade. As anxious as Jan was to begin to build his own home, it was decided that Jan and his family would stay with Stan a while longer, so the two brothers could get Stan's crops in first. Ben and Josie were assigned the job of clearing the parcel that was to comprise the homestead. This meant picking up rocks and fallen timber. Not easy work for relatively young children, but they were happy to help if it meant getting a home of their own. Ben was allowed to finish out the school year, but each spare minute was spent on the land. As summer approached, Emilia transplanted some perennials and seedlings from her sister-in-law's flower garden, around 𝕿𝖍𝖊 𝕽𝖊𝖉 𝖅 sign Ben had made for their land. I am here. This is mine.

JOSIE

As a girl of thirteen, Josie was caught between feeling like a woman and a child. Certainly she had the responsibilities of a woman, doing chores, sewing, mending and childcare. Her body informed her she was maturing. Part of her, however, longed to be a child, swimming in the pond, running barefoot in the soft grasses, and singing. She did not remember much of her own mother as she was so young when she died. Emilia had always been kind to her; only eleven years older, she was perhaps more like an older sister. Josie knew she was not a pretty girl having a plain face, grey eyes, and large nose. Her hair unlike her half- sister's, was straight and straw-like. Never having seen a picture of her mother, she assumed she must resemble her. Her schooling in Poland lasted only about three years. After that, she was needed at home to help care for the little ones. She could read and write, but only in Polish. The younger children seemed to pick up the new language more quickly. The only exposure she had to others her age was Sundays in church. Josie felt awkward, unintelligent and homely by comparison. Because only Polish was spoken at home, it was difficult for her to cultivate new language skills. Most of Sunday Mass was in Latin, so that did not help much. Emilia, perhaps feeling much the same, tried to help by braiding her step-daughter's long hair, and by sewing colorful babushkas for the two to wear to services, from scraps in Genja's sewing basket. Nothing went to waste in the Zalewski households, not even the smallest scrap of cotton. Josie had a knack for using scraps and castoffs to recreate useful and decorative items, such as pot holders, blankets or quilts. Fellow churchgoers often admired her crocheted hats and gloves worn in winter.

By the time she was sixteen, her father's farm was established. They had built a two story farmhouse, with a bedroom for Emilia and Papa, a kitchen, dining and living rooms on the first floor, and two large bedrooms on the second for the children to share. Josie thought it a grand house; better than anything she remembered in Poland. She did not care that she had to share a room with her sisters. The home was cozy and well-built with help from Uncle Stan and other neighbors around them. Many of the building supplies were ordered from the Sears-Roebuck Company, and were delivered by train from Chicago to Stevens Crossing, where Papa and Uncle Stan picked them up on Stan's flatbed wagon. What a country!

Josie awoke with the rooster each morning, dressed quickly, ran to the outdoor privy, and then proceeded to start breakfast. By this time, a new little sister Vladja (or *Gladys*) had joined the family, and Josie was most definitely her "little mother". Not only was she taken by the adorable little bundle, but little Stan was still a baby himself, and Emilia had her hands full. After the dinner dishes were washed, and the little ones put to bed, Josie fell into bed each night exhausted. At sixteen, little time for dreaming of parties, dances, lovely frocks or boyfriends.

The winter of their fourth year in America, their parish hosted their annual Christmas social and dance. Their family had never attended before, having felt awkward in their appearance and lack of English speaking skills. However, by this time they had all acquired some knowledge of the new language, and Emilia and her *Singer* had provided some new outfits for Christmas. Emilia braided the front of Josie's hair and pinned it up attractively, with the back hanging softly down her back, even adding a sprig of holly from their bushes. When she and Jan married, her new husband presented her with a Polish amber bead necklace. The fact that it had belonged to his first wife, Josie's mother, did not diminish its beauty. As she placed it around Josie's neck she hoped Viola was looking down with pride. The young girl caught her reflection in the mirror, and decided she did not look too bad in her new blue flowered dress. Her step-mother was not unaware of Josie's coming-of-age. She, herself, had married at sixteen. It was time for Josie to find a husband. Perhaps she could meet someone at the Parish social.

There were certainly no shortage of young men in the parish. Luckily, the day of the social was bright and sunny, unlike the wintry Wisconsin storms during the previous week. Each family was asked to contribute a food item to be shared if affordable. Josie and Emilia made delicious chruscki with powdered sugar, a kind of Polish, knotted fried doughnut, for which they received many compliments! The littlest ones seemed to enjoy the novelty of running and playing with others their age. The adults talked crops, the price of feed and of course, impending war in Europe. Many of the teens seemed awkward and shy. Those that lived "in town" and went to school regularly, seemed to know each other, and talked casually and joined in the dancing. The "farm kids" did not have that opportunity. They barely knew their neighbors, and did not have the time for any socializing. Josie was envious of the other girls' lighthearted, carefree manner, not to mention their "modern" clothing and bobbed hairstyles. The only dancing she had ever done were polkas with her family in the parlor on special occasions when Uncle Stan brought his fiddle. She stayed near Ben and her cousins. Ben loved to dance, and was very good at it. When a lively polka struck up at the social, Ben grabbed Josie and pulled her to the dance floor of the parish basement. At first she was mortified to dance in front of everyone, but because Ben was such an animated, talented lead partner, soon the other dancers on the floor parted and began to clap as Ben and Josie captivated the crowd. Emilia and Jan beamed. When the dance ended, a blushing Josie returned to the company of her cousins. A new boy had joined their group. Cousin Mykiel introduced him as Josef Milewski. The Milewski farm was about three miles from theirs. Mykiel remembered Joe from school, and had run into him sometimes in town at the General Store or Mill. Joe was fair skinned, light haired, slender and tall.

Joe complimented Ben and Josie on their polka. To her astonishment, Joe then asked Josie to dance. Other than her family, Josie had never danced with a boy. Before she could refuse, Joe caught her arm and led her onto the floor. He was not nearly as good a dancer as Ben, but she found herself enjoying the polka, even the unfamiliar touch of Joe's arm around her waist, and hand in hers. Luckily the lively steps did not allow for conversation. She was still so uncomfortable with her English! When it was over he said, "Dziekuje", (*thank you* in Polish), and, "Mito mi cie pozbac" (*it was nice to meet you here*).

That night all Josie could think about was Joe. She tried to recall his face. What color were his eyes? What was he wearing? The touch of his hand in hers. Did she make a fool of herself? She finally fell asleep reflecting on what she believed to be the best day of her life.

BEN

As far back as he could remember, Ben had always been fascinated with "things" and the way they looked. He loved the nearby meadow flowers for their lovely shapes and colors, but also how they played against the rusty wagon wheel abandoned there and the bright blue sky. Birds fascinated him, too. The brilliant blue-green of the mallards, and the graceful curves of the lake swans. He seemed to have a knack for rendering objects in pencil as well, and often drew patterns on cloth for mother or the girls to embroider. What he found particularly enjoyable was whittling wood. He found he could create sweet replicas of the birds and small creatures. His "hobby", however, often got him in trouble with Pa, who would reprimand him for not being busy at his chores, instead.

Like his mother, his love of flowers and color, helped make the Zalewski farmstead quite lovely, especially in late June when the daylilies, daisies, bachelor buttons and black-eyed susans were in full bloom. Emilia and some of the other Polish women of the parish, would trade flower cuttings and seeds. She was especially proud of the "passion flower" vine that she cultivated by the road. It wound itself around the signpost Ben had made denoting the Zalewski farm. Mother explained to the children why it was called a passion flower and pointed out the resemblances to Jesus' suffering on Good Friday, in the intricate lavender and red blooms with a "cross" at its center. Ben made it his mission to make sure the farmhouse was never in need of paint, and that thistles and weeds did not stand a chance in their flower garden. How Pa wished he paid as close attention to the vegetables and other crops in the fields! Nonetheless, they were all proud of the farm.

After a few years of hard work, the Zalewski farm began to turn a profit. One of the highlights of Ben's young life was the day he saw his first motion picture show. After a particularly hard week of harvesting, Pa decided to reward his oldest children with a picture show in Stevens Crossing. The theater was relatively new, and the "talk of the town". Ben was enamored with the beautiful people on the silent screen, their stylish costumes and automobiles, the way they danced and the music of the accompanying theater organ. He was hooked-on-Hollywood. Not much printed material made it to the farm via mail, but he read the little that was published about "the stars" in the Stevens Crossing Journal. On days Pa went to the General Store, Ben begged to ride along so he could page through the glossy magazines featuring pictures of his movie idols. His favorite was an actress of Polish descent named Pola Negri, a femme fatale, mistress to Charlie Chaplin and Rudolph Valentino! (In fact, when Ma and Pa's last child was born, Ben begged them to name her Pola, which they did!)

After completing third grade, Ben no longer went to school. He was needed on the farm. Unfortunately, although his English had improved, his grammar had not. The teen loved composing stories and plays that would feature his Hollywood matinee idols, but the lack of a more extensive English vocabulary and proper grammar frustrated him.

How he longed to see the world outside Stevens Crossing. When rumors of War spread, he almost wished he could be part of the new Selective Service Act created to increase America's forces should they go to war with Germany … at least he could leave the farm. The Great War as it was called, consumed all the talk around town. Most of the immigrant population were against it, having left Europe to avoid it. When German U-boats sunk the British ship, *Lusitania,* in May of 1915, killing 128 US citizens, War was soon declared, and men between the ages of 21 and 30 were required to register for the draft. Ben was just 17, but his two older cousins had to register. They were not called up. Josie's new husband, Joe, was drafted and sent to France. She wrote to him every day. One day a postcard arrived to the farm, addressed to Josie from Joe. It was white silk with a large avenging angel embroidered on it in black with the words, *A Souvenir of the World War*. Josie cried when Emilia put it on the mantle. The family prayed three Hail Mary's in front of it each evening before dinner for Joe's safe return.

BERNICE AND HELEN

Bronislawa, or Bernice, as her American friends called her, remembered very little of her immigration to America. She was just four. The farm near Stevens Crossing was her home. Her mother, Emilia, insisted Polish be spoken at home, but outside of the home, she struggled to speak the English she heard at school and in town. Her brother, Ben, seemed to be able to pick up the English words at a faster pace, and often helped her and Josie understand.

Bernice was what one might call "a beautiful baby", with a round face, large eyes and a full head of thick light curls. Josie was less of a big sister to her and baby Helena, and more of a little mother. Emilia was often weakened with morning sickness, or busy nursing the latest member of the Zalewski clan. By the time she started school, in addition to Helena, was Stanislaus and infant Vladja. Bernice liked being at school. The classroom was warm and orderly, and it was nice to be with other children besides her own family. She was not shy, like Josie, but outgoing and friendly, and did not seem bothered by older ones teasing her about her poor English. Cooking seemed to be her talent, especially baking. She learned early from Aunt Genja and Emilia. From Josie, she learned needlework, and when she was just ten, she crocheted an elegant new coverlet for her parent's bed.

Like the other children, she had more than her share of chores around the farm. As she got older, she spent more and more time helping with the smaller ones. Someone always needed changing which meant there were always diapers to be washed and dried. In the summer this did not seem as terrible to the young girl, but in the brutally cold Wisconsin winters, the wash water never seemed hot enough to cut the chill of the covered porch where the wash tub sat. She and Helena, her closest sibling in age, became inseparable. Every morning after hastily getting dressed, the two trod off to the hen house to gather eggs. Again, this was especially difficult for the two little girls when the winter snows hit. They would often wait until Pa and Ben had left for the barn and forged a path for them in the deep snow. Thankful for the heavy wool socks Josie had made for them, they made their way to the barn. Although not warm, the barn provided protection from the brutal wind and snow. The real reward, after the chore was complete, was a cup of steaming creamy milk, and fresh eggs cooked in bacon fat. Like her older siblings, Bernice was allowed to go to school and complete third grade. Although she missed school, and being around other children, she was not the best student and struggled with English, especially reading.

Helena, on the other hand, seemed to pick up her second language more easily, and was obviously bright. She loved reading, and her teacher, perhaps sensing her burgeoning intellect, often lent her books to take home which she avidly read by candlelight in their bed. A bit more sensitive than her older sister, Bernice, she was a willing helper, and never seemed to complain about the never-ending list of chores. She was a bit of a "mama's girl", and her favorite time of day, was when the family gathered after supper to pray the rosary. Helena loved the colored, faceted prayer beads and the pretty statue of the Virgin Pa had gotten for Emilia one Christmas; in truth, mama's old picture of the Black Madonna scared her a bit. During the warmer months, she made sure there were always flowers near the Madonna. A lovely voice, Helena sang in the church choir. About two years after baby Vladja was born, mama found herself again with child. The baby girl was born during the cold January winter. The home, although cozy, was small for the growing family, now with seven children. The new infant slept in Mama and Papa's bed, between them to keep warm, and to make it easier for Mama to nurse.

They were all heartbroken and tearful, as they laid their first family member to rest in America, in the cemetery adjacent to their Parish church. Pa and Ben fashioned a small cross from limestone as a marker. The new infant, just a few weeks old, had died in her sleep. Pa and Mama blamed themselves, perhaps fearing they had suffocated her unknowingly between them in their bed. Part of Mama died that day, too. Helena, especially noticed the change in her mother's demeanor, and could sense the chill between her and Papa. It was as if a dark cloud hung over the Zalewski home. Helena often saw Emilia silently weeping as she performed her motherly duties. Helena's heart ached for her mother, and she prayed to the Madonna to lift the burden of sorrow. The parish rallied, even in the cold, wintry weather to attend the funeral service, and provide meals for the grieving family. Infant mortality was high at this time, and many other families unfortunately knew the pain they were experiencing.

STAN AND GLADYS

Stanley, Stanislas in Polish, was the first American-born child in the family; finally, another male sibling thought Ben! Perhaps another boy to share the burden of farming chores. He somewhat resembled Ben with his features, but was not tall and lean like Ben, but stockier and shorter in build. He was the funny one in the family, always quick with a smile or a joke. He proved to be a great help to Pa and Ben, and seemed especially adept at machinery, how it worked, and how to repair it when needed. The years after the Great War, saw a substantial increase in production and use of farming implements. Although expensive, one piece of equipment was often shared by many of the neighboring farmers. The International Harvester *Farmall* tractor was life-changing. Stan was often called to other farms to help with the often finicky machinery. For this he sometimes garnered an extra coin, or perhaps a chicken or some vegetables.

One thing he did not like, however, was his "nickname". Partly because he was often confused with his uncle, Stan, and partly because he was being teased by his big brother, he was christened *Fritz*; a name picked up in a newspaper article about the Germans that Ben read. Although he hated it, especially during the war years, it stuck, and he took it with his usual good humor, and often made himself the butt of *Kraut jokes*. Wisconsin, especially the Milwaukee area, had huge German immigrant populations. During WW I, anti-German sentiment was especially high. The popular local tavern on the square in Stevens Crossing even changed its name from Schmidts to Smiths. The happiest day of his young life was the day Pa and

Uncle Stan bought their first car. Although it was used, and not shiny new, Fritz thought it the finest machine he had ever seen.

Vladja, or Gladys in English, was just a year younger that Stan, and they were often mistaken for twins. Gladys, however was the apple of her big brother Ben's eye. He gave much attention to her when she was a tot, especially after the new baby died, and Ma was somewhat despondent. She was a beautiful girl with an aptitude for cooking, and had similar interests as Ben. She loved to pour through the movie magazines when she could, loved setting a pretty table and arranging flowers for Ma. Gladys, although not as adept a seamstress as Ma or Josie, always seemed to pick the most fashionable fabric. Her hair was always neatly braded or brushed, and embellished with some bow or flower. Ben taught her to dance almost as soon as she could walk. As Helen was the student, Gladys was the diva. This is not to say she couldn't pull her weight around the farm. She had boundless energy, and had no problem killing and de-feathering a chicken, dressing a deer, or cleaning a fish. In later years they would recall that *Gladys always had a flair.*

LAWRENCE, VALENTINE AND HENRY

About two years after the death of infant Anna, Emilia gave birth to another son, Wojciech, or Lawrence. He was like another version of Ben, physically. Tall, lean, nice looking. Although he looked like his big brother, he was more akin to his big sister, Helena in spirit. Like her, he was a very spiritual child, devoutly praying his rosary each evening, serving Mass on Sundays, and volunteering to walk the long way to church to serve at funeral or wedding Masses when needed. He had two other passions, reading and fishing. He could often be seen with a fish pole in one hand, and a book in the other…dutifully only if and when he had finished his chores. Pa had quite the temper of late, softened a bit when presented with a nice stringer of brook trout or blue gill.

His teacher, like Helen's, saw intelligence in Lawrence, and sent him home from school with books she lent him. The teacher convinced Ma and Pa to let Lawrence continue past third grade, as she saw educational potential, possibly teaching in his future. Pa was not sure, but he had Ben and Stan to help in the fields, so he agreed. Helen often read to him as a child, and seemed to be his boon companion, therefore it nearly broke his heart when Helen announced she was leaving the family to enter the convent of the Sacred Heart Sisters in nearby Polonia. Ma and Pa were so proud. It seemed only natural to them that she enter the sisterhood, as she was such a sweet, spiritual girl, with many talents to share with others. Being a good student, the convent would afford her the formal education, life on the farm could not. The order was founded by Polish immigrants to America, so Helen would fit in nicely. Lawrence decided to study hard, and perhaps pursue the priesthood, himself when he was old enough.

On February 14, 1914, Aunt Genja helped Emilia usher in the newest addition to the family, a healthy boy. Having made his arrival on this most auspicious day, they named him Walentyna, or Valentine. Val as he was called by his siblings, was perhaps physically, the most striking in physical features, with piercing blue eyes, thick, dark curls, and finely chiseled features. He was neither thin like Lawrence, nor stocky like Fritz. In later years, movie-buff Ben, would call him "Valentino"…after the leading man and matinee idol, Rudolph Valentino! Although he pretended to be insulted, he was well aware of his good looks, and secretly relished the comparison. Unlike his brother Ben, he loved farming. He was enamored by the agricultural science of how things grew; what could be done to the soil to enrich it, which crops should be rotated, how best to irrigate. He could take or leave the animals, but loved the fields. Fairly good at math, he and Lawrence helped Pa with pricing and yields.

A turning point came for Val as a teenager, when Stan drove him to see the opening of a new airstrip at the nearby National Guard training facility. He had never seen an airplane "up-close and personal". He was hooked. The pilots looked so important in their leather helmets and silk scarves as they climbed out of their machines. What must it be like to see the fields from the air? He had read in Pa's farming journals about crop dusting; pilots who crossed the fields at low level, in modified old warbirds, dropping their loads of fertilizer, pesticides and even seeds. Proponents believed it would revolutionize farming. He vowed then and there that somehow he would learn to fly.

Val's *sidekick* turned out to be his little brother, Henz, or Henry. Eighteen months younger, he was the spitting image of his sibling. Same good looks, with an extremely sweet nature, like Helen or Lawrence in that respect. Unlike Val, Henry did not sulk during Mass, or complain at rosary time, but was prayerful and warmhearted. What they did share was their love of the land. Like Lawrence, Henry adored fishing, and like Stan, he loved cars.

One day while running after a stray cat, he tripped over a tree stump and chipped his front tooth. Ma soothed him as best she could assuring him it was just a "baby tooth" and would soon be replaced by a fine new one. The older children could not refrain from teasing him about his peculiar smile however, and promptly nicknamed him *Chip*.

WANDJA

The last child to bless the Zalewski household was a baby girl. Her full name was Amapola Wandja. Oldest brother, Ben, now 22, insisted she be named after the popular Polish film star, Pola Negri. Ma and Pa however, called her Wandja, and her now-Americanized siblings nicknamed her *Wendy*. Emilia was now over forty, Jan in his fifties. Large families were the norm at this time, especially it seemed in farming families, where every offspring was another pair of hands. By the time she arrived, Josie and Joe had already married, and had two infant sons, George and Henry. Joe's parent's grew tomatoes, and owned a canning factory nearby. The young couple had a small home of their own on the Milewski land near the cannery where Joe worked.

Bernice left the farm when she was sixteen, and moved to Chicago to find work as a domestic. The Windy City also had a huge Polish population, and someone in their parish had relatives there who helped her find work and a place to stay. This huge, bustling city was in a constant state of motion. After the Great Chicago Fire of the late 1800's, rebuilding the city was ever advancing, attracting the brightest new architects and builders, bankers and investors, as well as immigrants escaping the war and famines of Europe, hoping to get jobs in the reconstruction.

Not only did Bernice find a job, she made enough money to support herself as well as send a few dollars a month to Emilia and the family. She and her roommates at Mrs. Schula's boarding house on the South Side attended St. Jozafat's Parish Church each Sunday. It was here that she caught the eye of Jan, *Jack,* Glowacki. Rumors had it that the Glowacki's were related to Bartosz Glowacki, a storied war hero whose portrait was on Polish currency! Bernice was flattered that he had approached her after Mass one Sunday, and asked to walk her home. He, too, lived in the neighborhood, and had a custodial job with Illinois Bell. His family had immigrated a few years earlier than the Zalewski's. He spoke English well, and she was impressed with his good looks; not tall, but with curly, dark hair and deep brown eyes. He seemed so much more "worldly" than any of the farm boys from Wisconsin. After a short courtship, the two young people took the train to Stevens Crossing to ask Jan's blessing, and have a family wedding at the farm. Emilia was impressed with the store-bought wedding dress Bernice had borrowed from a friend in Chicago, in the new, short "flapper" style. She also had her beautiful thick hair cut in a "bob". Eleven year old Gladys was enamored with her glamourous city-sister. Jack, on the other hand, seemed like a fish-out-of-water at his bride's home, remembering little of farming life. He was surprised to see his new wife had such young siblings. He, himself, had only one brother from whom he was estranged. His new father-in-law was a bit intimidating; he did not see him smile until the wedding toast, when the beer and schnapps began to flow.

Josie was the Matron-of-Honor; Ben, Jack's Best Man. Beloved Helena was not able to attend, much to Bernice's disappointment as she was still in the novitiate of the Sisters of the Sacred Heart. Ben created a traditional flower crown and fragrant bouquet from the Zalewski garden. Jack had to agree that the wedding feast was far better than anything he had had in Chicago. Local musicians performed and everyone did the Polka. No "city" music here. The day after the wedding was the traditional *poprawiny,* or "pop-and-wieners" as the children would call it, which was yet another reception to finish off the leftover food and drink.

Eighteen months after they were married, Bernice gave birth to their only son, Norbert. When baby Wandja was born, she already had three nephews older than she was. Emilia was disappointed she could not travel to Chicago to help her daughter through the birth, but she, herself, was not up to the journey. Bernice assured her she had friends and parishioners who would assist. The South Side after all, was a tight Polish community. It was a difficult birth, and after hours of severe labor, Bernice was transported to the hospital where doctors used forceps' to deliver the hefty, healthy baby boy. Unfortunately, infection set in, reproductive damage had occurred, and Bernice would not be able to have more children. Jack was relieved and thankful that his wife and son survived.

When baby Wendy was two, the family gathered at the nearby convent of the Sacred Heart Sisters to watch as Helena took her final vows to now become Sister Mary Philothea; named for an Eastern European monastic and martyr. The younger children, and later most everyone, would call her *Sr. Phil*. Emilia and Josie made her a beautiful white "bridal" gown for the ceremony with imported lace Bernice had sent from Chicago. Gladys cried when Helena, now Sr. Philothea, gave her a watch and a ring that she had been gifted from her parents as a teen, after she renounced all her worldly possessions as part of her commitment ceremony. Helena announced that the Provincial had assigned her to the motherhouse in Chicago, where she would continue her studies to become a teacher in one of the many parochial schools run by the Sisters. This was wonderful news for Bernice, having her cherished sister near her again.

Chip, as the second youngest, and big brother, took it upon himself to be little Wendy's teacher and guardian. She adored him, and followed like a puppy. She would later recall how in the worst of weather, Chip would always insist on going first to plow through the deep snows on their walk to school, so Wendy could walk safely in the tracks he made. He defended his little sister from Pa's increasingly bad temper, and often took the blame for mischief she caused, like the time she left the gate to the chicken coop ajar, and the creatures wandered everywhere, or when she ate Ma's freshly baked cake intended for the church supper. He was her super hero.

THE GREAT WAR AND
THE GREAT DEPRESSION

Everyone was overjoyed when Joe returned safely from *the- war- to-end-all- wars*. By the time he was trained and sent to France, the fighting was all but over, but the sight of the bombed-out villages, vile gas masks, and mutilated, wounded soldiers and displaced, often orphaned souls, was something he would never be able to erase from his consciousness. Nightmares were commonplace. He took refuge in his sweet family and two strong sons. His father's business at the canning factory was good, and after the War, there was great call for their product. Josie was a wonderful wife and mother, so talented at needlework that she was often sought after by locals to help with wedding and christening dresses and the like. During the War, she had knit and sent warm, wool caps and socks to her new husband for which he was grateful and envied. Shortly after Helena professed her vows, Josie found herself again with child. Maybe a girl this time.

The years after the War were relatively good for the Wisconsin farmers. Demand for dairy, and produce was high. The Zalewski's were able to afford a used automobile, and some farm machinery. After the harvest, Ben often travelled to spend the winter months in Chicago or Milwaukee, where he could find decent paying factory work. By now they had relatives in both places, where Ben could find temporary work and lodging. Every nickel helped. He saved as much as he could before grudgingly heading back to The Red Z in the spring to help put in the crops. He missed the big city life with its museums, shops, dance halls and picture shows. He knew however, he was born into farm life, and as the oldest son, it was his duty to return. Stan and Pa could handle the milking in the winter, but come planting time, all able hands were needed. He had so many ideas in his head from things he had gleaned in the city that oftentimes he was frustrated at the lack of time and resources he had to bring these ideas to fruition. For example, at the great Art Institute of Chicago, he had seen in the Asian galleries, huge Moorish inspired wooden screens. As an amateur woodcarver, the pierced wood technique and intricate motifs intrigued him. He tried to sketch them as best he could lest he forget when he returned home. He had so many questions; how he wished he could have stayed in Chicago, or at least completed more schooling when he was younger.

The 1920's were relatively good for the Zalewski's. The farm was productive, Josie, Bernice and Helena had moved away, and had lives of their own, hopefully without the same struggles their mother and father faced in their early years. Farming life was hard. These were the years before rural areas had electricity, central heat and telephone service. Winters were frigid and summers were humid, often sweltering, but there were always cows to be milked, eggs to be gathered, stock to feed and crops to pick. If you were not outside, you were inside where there was canning to be done, jams to boil, washing and hanging of clothing or sewing and mending of same. Feeding and cleaning up after a large family three times a day was work enough. Luckily, Emilia and Ben planted a large vegetable garden from their very first year in Stevens Crossing, which nourished them for most of the year. The younger children were taught weed-from-seed, as soon as they could manage to help, and the entire family took pride in this providential plot on the side of their home. Scraps and peelings, if not used to feed the pigs, were used to fertilize the garden. Nothing went to waste on their farm, and prayers of thanksgiving were offered up daily for their blessings. This practice would serve them well when The Great Depression hit America, in 1929.

The cities seemed more affected by the Stock Market crash than did the rural areas. Ben had been in Chicago on that black Tuesday in October. The factory where he worked closed the next day. Because of the run on the banks, he was denied his last paycheck. As much as he loved the big city, he was grateful to have 𝕿𝖍𝖊 𝕽𝖊𝖉 𝖅 to go back to. On the train ride home to Stevens Crossing, he pondered on his fellow workers at the plant, many of whom lived paycheck-to-paycheck, petrified at the prospect of providing food and rent for their families, with no income in sight. When Ben left Chicago, Jack, recently promoted, still had his job at Illinois Bell uncertain of course, how long it would last. Fear hung like a huge black storm cloud over the Windy City.

Ben arrived home to yet another disaster. The Milewski canning factory had been struck by lightning, and burned to the ground, along with Joe and Josie's house. No one was killed in the fire, but this tragedy could not have come at a more inopportune time. Not only were Joe and his family out of work, but so were all their employees. The physical damage to the factory structure was beyond repair. So many of the local farmers sold their tomatoes to the Milewski cannery! The misery trickled down. Josie was almost inconsolable; although thankful for the safety of her family, she saw all she and Joe had worked for reduced to ash. Her beautiful needlework spreads and linens! The exquisite oak cradle Ben had made for the babies. Emilia's heart broke for the young couple. They moved in with Joe's parents, but how long could they all survive?

The Milewski children would later recall how their mother would walk with them from farm to farm, mile upon mile, asking if they needed any help, farm work or domestic. Word had traveled quickly about the tragic fire, but the depression hit everyone hard. Neighbors and parishioners helped each other when they could. Josie was often given a jar of jam, chunk of cheese, or loaf of bread as she went from farm to farm with her children. If she were lucky, she was given an empty feed sack or two that she could use to make clothes for her children. The millers of flour and grain had taken to making their sacks in various prints as they knew many were forced to use the empty sacks for clothing or linens. This door-to-door *begging,* incensed Joe, but his mental state after the devastating fire, and the haunting horrors of The Great War, left him physically and emotionally impaired. His parents were getting older, too, and he had foolishly thought the cannery would provide for the family for generations.

Three years after the fire, Joe decided to take his wife and children to Chicago. Bernice had written that some were getting jobs created by the city. Most involved working on infrastructure. Joe had worked at the cannery running the day-to-day office operations, but was no stranger to physical labor, and would do anything to support his family, and keep his wife from supplicating. They could stay with Bernice and Jack until something was found. The Glowacki's home was not spacious by any means, but it had a large, and very dark basement. This subterranean zone would be home for the five Milewski's for six months.

Ben, Stan, and Lawrence, as the oldest siblings left on the farm, did what they could to make it through. Farmers were perhaps luckier than most in the fact that they at least had food for their own families. Their vegetable garden provided fresh produce in the spring through fall, and Emilia and the girls canned more to be used in the winter months. Their chickens provided eggs, and meat. Hogs provided meat and lard. Farm lunches often consisted of lard or mashed potato sandwiches. There was little grumbling. They knew they were perhaps luckier than most to be able to fill their bellies. Farmers bartered with each other as well; those who had eggs traded for flour and the like.

Emilia and the children noticed Jan becoming more and more withdrawn. When he did speak, it was in a very rough tone, and his temper was short, especially with the young ones. He had no patience for chores going undone, misbehavior or, worst of all, waste. His wife attributed it to the stress of the economic depression. He saw the price of corn, which had soared after the War, fall to 8 cents a bushel. Eggs were 6 cents a dozen. It took 100 pounds of milk to earn a dollar. Many farmers who saw the prosperity of the post War years, used their earnings to finance more machinery and/or land. Now threats of foreclosure and repossession loomed large. News of the horrid drought and record summer heat in the *dust bowl* of the Great Plains, made Midwestern farmers thankful for the ability to grow crops at all.

Ben, as the oldest, often got the brunt of Pa's anger. There was precious little time or money for any of the things Ben loved, films, dances, popular magazines and especially woodcarving. As Jan became more withdrawn, more of the work load fell to Ben, not only the physical work, but the book-keeping as well. Luckily Lawrence was good with numbers, and Emilia brilliant at stretching a nickel.

Lawrence, as the *smart one*, was allowed to go to high school. His teachers as well as Fr. Suleck, persuaded Jan and Emilia that he could become a fine teacher or perhaps enter the seminary. This meant he would have to attend a year at the teacher's college in Stevens Crossing. As teachers were in short supply in the area, his tuition would be covered by the State. Emilia managed to give him ten cents a week to cover his meals and incidentals while at school. He would sleep some nights in a friend's attic room when the weather was too bad to get back to 𝕿𝖍𝖊 𝕽𝖊𝖉 𝖅 after classes.

When news of the new federal program, the Civilian Conservation Corps, or CCC, hit the local papers, it was decided that Fritz would enlist at the local CCC camp in nearby Plover. Ben was too old to enlist, and Val too young. The Government created this *New Deal* program, modeled after a military organization, to give jobs to the unemployed. Enlisted men, ages 18-25, were paid $30. per month. It was required that most of this be sent home to their families. Food, uniforms, lodging (tents or barracks), medical, dental and barber services were provided at the various camps located throughout the states. CCC workers planted trees, helped to build dams and state parks, fought forest fires, and functioned in many other areas of environmental conservation, often depending on their location. Because of his love of automobiles and mechanics, Fritz was often assigned truck duty, as a driver or mechanic. The work was hard, especially in the freezing cold or sweltering sun, but he was used to hard work on the farm, unlike some of the city boys. Classes were set up at camp to teach reading and English to the illiterate. He actually made a life-long friend who would later introduce him to his future wife, and the extra dollars sent home were a blessing to the Zalewski's. Fritz stayed with the Corps two years.

With Fritz gone, and Lawrence at school most of the time, more and more responsibility for keeping the family afloat fell to Ben. Gladys helped Ma with the day-to-day chores of laundry, cleaning, gardening, preserving, butchering, mending and cooking. Ben counted on Val and Chip to help with the milking, animal care, planting and harvesting. They were young teens, but good and strong. On rare occasions, Ben and Gladys would go to a dance or picture show in town. He lived for these occasions, as his pretty sister was a good companion, and liked these things as much as Ben. They could lose themselves in the exploits of Rudolph Valentino and Errol Flynn, fanaticize about glamorous starlets like Pola Negri and Jean Harlow, or laugh at the antics of The Marx Brothers or Buster Keaton. For a nickel, they could see a cartoon, newsreel, perhaps a "B" movie and a feature film, escaping for a few hours the worries of the farm and the Depression. The two of them even won a couple of dance competitions. Pretty Gladys was a bit of a flirt, and the boys loved her, but Ben was the over-protective big brother, much to Gladys' dismay. She often teased him about not having a sweetheart of his own, but he said there was little time or money for courting. How could he consider having a family of his own when he was responsible for the lives and livelihood of his parents and siblings?

Ben felt the weight of the world on his shoulders. Frustration was consuming him. Something was definitely different with Pa. Moody and pensive, he took to drinking more and eating less. He was more often than not late for morning chores, and furious with the boys for seemingly no reason. Arguments with Ma became more prevalent. He was prone to stomp out of the house in a huff and walk to Uncle Stan's for a schnapps, coming home late and inebriated. Emilia was worried, but said nothing to Ben. Everyone was on edge. They were living a national nightmare. Hadn't they risked life and limb to escape Poland for a better life? Perhaps if he had not tasted life in Chicago with all the stuff of his dreams, Ben would not be so exasperated. When he thought of the galleries and museums, the theaters and finery in the shops there, he felt very discouraged and unfulfilled. He knew in his heart that he should be thankful that he had a roof over his head and food to put in his mouth. He could not help but feel he was destined for more than the life of a poor illiterate farmer. The worse Pa got, the more indignant Ben became, overwhelming feelings of unfairness seething inside him.

Needless to say, there was little money available for *luxuries* like new clothes, toys or games. There was little time to enjoy such pleasures, even if they were available. With his two older brothers away, and Pa not always well, Chip and Val were Ben's captives. First ones up to do the milking and let the cows to pasture; a quick mug of milk, and chunk of bread with Emilia's homemade jam, then to feeding the animals, and tending to the fields. With Pa's short temper, and Ben's escalating mean spirit, the boys dare not sleep in, or slip up, ever. The resulting wrath for such a transgression was wicked. Any spare time was often spent fishing or hunting for the supper table. Chip, like Lawrence, loved to fish. Perhaps because he could get lost in his thoughts and dreams, waiting for a bite from a record size trout. The bigger the fight they put up, the better he liked it. He also liked the look on Ma's face when he brought home such a prize. Val seemed to like hunting more, and was pretty good with Pa's rifle. Duck or pheasant was a delicacy, and also brought a needed smile to Ma's face, and one of pride to Pa's.

What Chip really wanted was a bicycle. The ones in Ma's Sears and Roebuck catalog were much too expensive, as were those he had seen in a storefront shop in town. He could picture himself on one, preferably a red *Schwinn* with lots of chrome detail, warm summer sun and cool breeze in his face, leading the cows to pasture, or running errands for Ma. He didn't dare approach Pa with the idea, and when he said something to Ben, his brother threw the rake in his hand at him, and proceeded to list all the things the family needed, least of all, a bicycle.

The Tzrebiatowski family owned the farm on the other side of Pa's. They, too, had emigrated from Poland, several years before the Zalewski's. They had three grown children, two of which were still living with their families on the land, helping "Mr. Tzreb". They had always been kind to the Zalewski's, especially when they first arrived, bringing milk for the children, and vegetables from their garden. Mrs. Tzreb brought cuttings from her perennials for Ma and Ben to plant in their flower beds. Mr. Tzreb and his boys helped Pa and Uncle Stan build the frame of the house, and, along with some others from St. Casmir's, raise the barn.

The Tzrebiatowski's had two automobiles, and were always generous about stopping by the Zalewski farm to see if Ma needed anything from town, or perhaps someone needed a lift, before they drove to Stevens Crossing or Mosinee. This was especially helpful in winter. Sometimes Mr. Tzreb would leave his farm early on especially cold days, so he could offer the younger Zalewski children a ride to school. He had a soft spot in his heart for young Chip and Wendy. They reminded him of his two youngsters who did not survive the Flu epidemic before the Great War. They were two little troopers, and never complained about their long walk to school. Mikel Tzreb got on well-enough with Pa, but there was little socializing. The Zalewski's kept to themselves or relatives.

Fritz often found himself at the Tzreb farm working on the automobiles. Although Mikel was willing to pay, Fritz was thrilled just to be near these machines. From Fritz, Mikel learned a lot about the Zalewski family as he chattered on while he worked on the cars. He had heard about the devastating fire at the cannery of course, and Fr. Suleck announced Helena's final profession of vows after Mass. Fritz filled him in on his plans to join the CCC, to earn some money to help support his younger siblings. Chip was also good with machinery, and Fritz suggested Mr. Tzreb call him if he needed work done on the automobiles after he left for Camp.

Word spread at St. Casmir's, as gossip often does, about Pa's drinking, and overall demeanor. Emilia often came to Mass with just the children, and made excuses for Jan's absence from church. Mikel Tzreb had heard from Fritz about altercations between Pa and Ben, and had seen these for himself on several occasions when he had stopped by to drop off some venison his boys had bagged, or things Emilia needed from town. Pa shrieked about not needing charity, and, "if Ben wasn't running the farm into the ground, they wouldn't be ashamed to face their neighbors." Mikel could see the loathing on Ben's face and the tears in Emilia's eyes. It was the Great Depression. Everyone's nerves were raw. Despair was rampant and not confined to this family. Although it hurt Mikel to see this, he understood.

After Fritz left for CCC camp, The Tzrebs did, indeed need some work done on the car. Mikel called on Chip who was happy to have an excuse to escape the tension at home and make a penny working at the Tzrebs. As he chatted with Mr. Tzreb on the way to his farm, Chip told him about how he wished he had a bicycle so he could ride over to the Tzrebs, or run errands for Ma. When they got to the farm, Mikel took Chip to his barn, and showed him an old bike that belonged to one of his sons. It was bent, and pretty rusted, also missing a wheel. Mr. Tzreb said Chip could have it and maybe fix it up in time. Young Chip was thrilled and thanked his benefactor over and over.

Not wanting to make a scene, and perhaps incur his father's wrath, Mikel and Chip carefully hid the bike in a corner of the Z barn and covered it with straw. The kind gentleman had also provided Chip with some sandpaper and steel wool to get started with the restoration. Any chance he got, Chip was working away on that bike. One day shortly thereafter, Chip was fishing with his big brother Lawrence, and confided in him about the bike. Perhaps because they had a splendid catch that afternoon, but more probably because he had such a big and generous heart, Lawrence offered to give Chip a penny of his ten cent allowance each week that Ma provided for teacher's college. Lawrence could make-do. The bicycle needed a new chain and a new tire. He would have to save for over a year and hope Mr. Tzrebs needed more car repairs. With luck, he could maybe get used parts more cheaply. God bless Lawrence.

It did, indeed take Chip almost two years to save for the parts. Mr. Tzreb's son found him a chain off an old bike at a junk site in Stevens Crossing, and purchased the new tire for him with the pennies he saved. Lots of elbow grease took off most of the rust, and Chip was able to find some red paint for the fenders. It was certainly not the pretty streamline *Schwinn* in the catalog, but it worked, and it was his pride and joy. By some miracle, his secret project was never discovered by Pa or Ben. He was careful not to tell his sisters either, lest they let it slip. Everyone was going to be so surprised when he rode it out of the barn to lead the cows to pasture. He was now fifteen.

The day of Chip's big reveal dawned clear and bright. He sprang out of bed without being called, and rushed to the barn to do the milking and feed the animals. While he ate his breakfast, he noticed Pa was absent from the table again, and Ben was particularly quiet and ill-tempered. Ma looked like she had been crying. Chip knew better than to ask any questions, besides, nothing could spoil this day for him. How proud Ben would be to see what his little brother had accomplished. Just think of the time it will save around the farm, getting to and from the pastures and fields. Ben abruptly got up from the table, uncharacteristically leaving most of the food on his plate, grabbed his hat and bellowed for Chip and Val to follow. The boys followed him toward the barn where Ben shouted for them to get the cows out to pasture. Chip told Val he'd be along shortly, and went to his hiding place and uncovered his treasure.

Never had he been so excited and proud. He couldn't wait to see his brother's faces when he rode out of the barn. Chip carefully removed the straw covering, and dusted off his prize possession. He could hear Ben hollering for him outside. The time had come, after almost two years. Chip hopped on the bike and rode towards Ben's shadow framed by the open barn door. For the rest of his life, he would never forget the scenario that followed. "Where did you get that?" Ben screamed. Chip's voice quivered as he told Ben the story about Mr. Tzrebs gift and his two years of saving. He didn't dare mention Lawrence's part. Instead of being proud of the young entrepreneur, Ben launched into a tirade, screaming how every penny counted, and how dare he just think of himself above the welfare of his family. He called his younger brother worthless and lazy. Inexplicably, Ben picked up the long handled axe that was sitting just inside the barn door, and began hacking away at the cherished bicycle. With hot tears streaming down his cheeks, Chip bolted from the barn, down the drive past the faded *Red Z* sign, and did not stop running until he was on the county road leading to town.

Shoeless, he did not even feel the stones beneath his feet. He felt nothing. Aimless, he did not care what happened to him, he just knew he would never go back to the farm. The boy didn't remember how far he walked that morning, but the sound of Mr. Tzrebs pickup truck slowing down beside him, caused him to stop momentarily. One look at the boy's face, and Mikel Tzrebs knew something was terribly wrong. Mikel persuaded Chip to hop in the car, as he was going into Stevens Crossing for supplies. The young man was silent but for the sniffles and tears that streamed down his face. When they got to town, Mr. Tzrebs parked in front of the feed store, and asked Chip if he wanted to talk. The story poured forth like a burst dam, breaking Mikel's heart upon hearing it. Always having a soft spot for the young Zalewski children, and having heard the rumors of Jan's erratic behavior, and Ben's callous attitude, Mikel questioned Chip about what he could do to help.

Right next to the feed store was a storefront that served as an enlistment office for the Civilian Conservation Corps, the New Deal program that Fritz had joined. The large recruitment poster in the window featured a handsome, smiling, young man, holding, of all things, an axe. Was this an omen? *"The CCC—A young man's chance to work, to live, to learn, to build, and to conserve our natural resources."* He would enlist. That would show Ben how lazy and good-for-nothing he was! Let him run things with one less pair of hands! Ma would have one less mouth to feed, and the $20.00 a month he could send home each month, certainly would prove his worth. Other than missing Ma and his younger siblings, he didn't care if he ever saw the place again. The problem was, the enlistment age was eighteen. Chip was fifteen. He had nothing but the clothes on his back; not even shoes!

Because so few immigrants at that time had any kind of formal identification, recruitment offices such as this relied on the signature of a parent or witness in regards to proof of age. Mikel, unsure of Chip's decision, took Chip into the dry goods store, and bought him a pair of socks and work shoes. He would be provided with uniforms and personal toiletries if accepted by the Corps. After buying the boy a sandwich and something to drink, he again questioned Chip's decision. If Mikel would not help him get into the Corps, he would otherwise make his way, but he would NEVER return to the farm. So in the early afternoon of the day the young man had so eagerly awaited, Mr. Mikel Tzrebs witnessed that Henry *Chip* Zalewski was indeed eighteen years of age, and now had to forfeit the remaining few years of his youth, and become a man.

Finding him healthy, strong and in need, they indeed enlisted the boy into the Corps, beginning immediately. He was transported to the nearby Training Camp in Plover, with two others who had signed up that day. One of them Chip recognized from St. Casmir's. He hoped he would not spill the beans about him being underage. Because the young men were all from desperate situations, Chip's appearance, and lack of personal items, was not that unusual. He did not believe he would run into Fritz, as he had been sent to a camp in the northern part of the state. In Plover, the new recruits were issued a cardboard container containing two uniforms, a coat, hat, gloves, two pair of socks, and work boots. They were also given a toothbrush, and other personal items in a small leather case. The CCC boys in Plover, were housed in one of two large barracks, with rows of military-style cots. Having been assigned a bunk, Chip was told gear was to be stored under his cot. Meals were served in another barracks that served as the mess hall, medical services building and Post Exchange, where they could buy incidentals and cigarettes. He really did not have time to reflect on the day's events, or what would come next.

The camp was run very much like an Army boot camp; calisthenics at dawn before breakfast, followed by briefings on the day's assigned duties and more PT. This group of recruits was being trained to work at a new State Park being developed at Rib Mountain, not too far west of them. They would help build roads and trails, plant trees and shrubs, construct park buildings and outdoor furniture, as well as clean and groom the waterways. It was good to be away from the farm and on his own. He felt sense of pride and solidarity he had never experienced before.

Chip wrote to Ma to assure her he was OK. He wasn't sure how much, if any of the story was relayed to her from Mikel Tzrebs. He was able to get post cards from the PX, and tried to write a few lines to Ma every week. His brother, Lawrence, sent him letters every so often to keep him apprised on the situation at home. Ben had informed him about Chip's sudden exodus, after Lawrence saw the battered remains of Chip's bike. Lawrence was his lifeline, yet again. He filled him in on news of the girls and their families in Chicago. It seems Joe Milewski was able to get a clerk's job with the city. It helped that he had experience with this while working at his father's cannery.

Jack Glowacki still had his maintenance job with the telephone company. Illinois Bell was solvent, even during the Depression years. Bernice was able to see her beloved Helen, now Sr. Philothea, as she was assigned duty at a nearby orphanage. Fritz had one more year of duty with the CCC, and Gladys had secured a position in Milwaukee, as a live-in cook for a wealthy family of Polish descent. Val continued to help Ben on the farm, as Jan seemed to be getting worse, and another man was needed, especially with Chip gone, Fritz away, and Lawrence in school most of the time. Val secretly envied Chip being away seeing more than the five square miles surrounding their farm. He decided when Fritz returned, he was going to enlist in the army, and learn to fly.

There were always rumors of war, especially in letters Ma received from her relatives in Poland. Until the Great War, the country was divided, with three nations trying to swallow them up. Their national independence was hard-fought and short-lived. As bad as America was during The Depression, at least there was peace. Letters speculated that perhaps Russia would swoop in from the East, and set up a Communist regime. German waves of anti-Semitism were flooding in from the West. Ma cried when she read these letters, fearful for those loved ones there. Emilia cried a lot lately.

Shortly after Chip left, Jan disappeared. He left after breakfast with his rifle. All assumed he was going hunting, although he was barefoot. By this time, Emilia knew to just let him be. When he wasn't home by dark, Val was sent to Uncle Stan's to look for him, however Stan had not seen him all day. The young man then went to the Tzreb farm to check and even drove through Stevens Crossing checking in at taverns he might have stopped at. No one had seen Jan in town, either. It was a long and sleepless night for the family, fearing the worst. Perhaps a hunting accident or bear attack? It was a cool evening and Jan was not properly dressed. At dawn on horseback, Ben headed out to the woods Jan favored for hunting. Val got in the jalopy and slowly drove the backroads looking, and questioning neighbors along the way. On the afternoon of the third day, a police car drove up to the farm. They had found Jan sleeping along the side of the road, at the edge of the woods. He was incoherent. The officers, seeing he had no identification, took him to the hospital in Stevens Crossing, where they treated him for exposure, and dehydration. Luckily, one of the nurses remembered Val stopping by the day before, and inquiring about his missing father and had left his name and address. Things continued to decline after that day. Jan was prone to wandering, so someone had to keep eyes on him all day. Although he was strong, and could still perform farm chores, he often left things half-done or forgot what he was supposed to do. He called Wendy, Josie, and Val, Stan. Saddest of all, he referred to Emilia as Viola, the name of his first wife, He never spoke English, and did not understand it at all when spoken to him. Ben felt the enormity of this added strain. It hurt him deeply to watch his rock of a father crumble before his eyes, and see what this was doing to his mother.

INTERVENING YEARS

ritz returned to the farm after his three years with the CCC were over. Needless to say, he was shocked to see how Pa had deteriorated. In fact, Pa did not recognize him. It broke his heart. The rest of the family praised his efforts while away, and told him how much they needed and appreciated the funds he sent home every month. Ma, of course, thought he looked thin. Wendy thought his new moustache and uniform made him look debonair. He boasted about the skills he had acquired, and some of the classes he had taken to improve his English. But most of all, he talked about his CCC buddy, Piotr Babiak. He was from near-by Mosinee, a farming community, to the east of them. Piotr had a photo of his sister, Jean, with whom Fritz had begun corresponding, using the new English language skills he had acquired at camp.

After Fritz had been home about a week, he did a major tune-up on the old family jalopy, and decided to take it for a spin. It was early October, and the majority of the harvest was done. It was a cool afternoon and the trees were putting on their annual autumnal show of brilliant color. No one expected the snow. Fritz had driven to Mosinee to visit Piotr and perhaps finally meet his "pen-pal", Jean. She was prettier than her picture, tall and lithe, with a lovely smile and shoulder-length brown waves. He was smitten. Mrs. Babiak served coffee and cake, and they all chatted and recounted stories of their time at the CCC camp. Hours passed, and no one paid any attention to what was happening outside. When Fritz left to drive back to the farm, there was a light dusting of snow everywhere. As the sun went down, the rate of snowfall increased. Slush quickly became ice. The tires on the old jalopy were threadbare.

Fritz woke up in a hospital bed two days later. The old car had skidded on an icy curve near Uncle Stan's farm, and hit a bank of oak trees. Luckily, Stan had heard the loud sound of the crash, and came running out to investigate the reason. He could smell the smoke from his front door, so he grabbed his coat and hat, and headed toward the source of the acrid smell. Through the heavy snowfall, he could see the smoldering outline of a vehicle. As he approached, he could see what appeared to be a body lying a few feet from the wreckage. Fritz had been thrown from the vehicle on impact. When Stan turned the man over, he was horrified to see the victim was his nephew and namesake. After carefully dragging the body away from the car for fear of fire, he ran back up the driveway to his home and yelled for his son to dress and harness the horses to the wagon. Miraculously, the young man was alive, and not bleeding too badly. The snow had begun to dissipate, and Stan, his son, and the horse-drawn wagon made its way to Stevens Crossing hospital.

Fritz spent over two weeks in the hospital recovering. He had a broken, arm, wrist, ribs and severe bruising. Several deep wounds had to be stitched as well, especially on his right leg. The old jalopy was beyond repair. Word spread quickly of the accident, prompting a welcome hospital visit from Piotr and Jean. Tearfully, she promised to write to him once he got back to the Zalewski farm to recover.

Her letters were the spark he needed to heal. He was at first, overcome with guilt for having ruined their source of transportation, the cost of the medical bills, and Ben having lost yet another set of hands running the farm. Partly because he broke his right arm and wrist, and partly because he was not very eloquent at writing love letters, he had Wendy answer Jean's letters for him, which she was happy to do, being quite the romantic, and young match-maker.

Fritz and Jean were married in 1941, just prior to America's involvement in World War II. Piotr was best man, Jean's oldest sister, Anne, was Matron-of-honor.

DEPRESSION LIFE
IN THE CITY

Gladys missed her family, but felt she could help them more by earning a good wage in Milwaukee, and sending most of her earnings home. She was a "live-in" second cook, for the Wehr family, originally from German-occupied Poland. They were now second-generation Americans. Mr. Wehr's father had begun an iron ore, and later steel parts manufacturing factory in Milwaukee. Although they, too, faced hard times during the Depression, they had already accumulated great wealth, certainly enhanced by the need for metal parts during The Great War. Franklin Roosevelt's New Deal program boosted steel production, as their product was needed to build the infrastructure this program was designed for.

Mrs. Anna Wehr, having had a privileged up-bringing as the daughter of a Milwaukee banker, entertained lavishly and often. She adored Gladys, as she was lively, pretty and had an innate sense for making even the plainest of "depression fare" look most appetizing.

Gladys loved arranging the table centerpieces and using the beautiful silver and tableware they owned. She had never seen such finery, and didn't even mind polishing the beautiful metal serving pieces. Mrs. Wehr reveled in the compliments she received after one of her soirees.

Gladys had been working for the Wehr's for just over a year. One evening she woke from a deep sleep in excruciating pain. Her poor room-mate, not knowing what to do, awakened Mrs. Wehr. Gladys was doubled over on the bed. Luckily, the Wehrs had telephone service, and called for an ambulance. Less than an hour later, Gladys had emergency surgery to remove a very large cyst that had ruptured in her abdominal area. When she came to, she vaguely remembered the doctor telling her what had happened, and that it involved her ovaries. She thought she saw tears in Mrs. Wehr's eyes. Unfortunately for the naïve farm-girl, she did not understand the implications of this procedure until much later. Everyone assured her she was young and would recover quickly, which she did. Her employers could not have been nicer.

It was rare that Gladys had an evening off, but when she did, she and one of the housemaids she shared a room with, Blanche, would head to the movies, or to a parish dance. It was at one of these dances, that she and Blanche met the Rogalinski brothers, Albin and Harold. They both had dark, wavy hair and bright blue eyes. The four of them danced for hours and then stopped at a nearby tavern for a nightcap. The boys were embarrassed they could not afford the cover charge to take them to one of the fancy new nightclubs that had sprung up after Prohibition had ended. When *Al and Harry* walked the girls back to their elegant digs on Lakeshore Drive, for an instant the two girls felt like Cinderella's. The bubble burst quickly as they confessed that they were only the hired help. After that night, whenever they were free, the four of them were inseparable. They all had so much in common, mainly their Polish-Catholic immigrant status. The foursome spent a lot of time playing cards and board games, and going to dances and festivals usually at a local church. On rare occasions, Mrs. Wehr would pass on to Gladys theater or concert tickets she would not be using. The girls usually went together, as the guys were embarrassed by their lack of proper dress. They were lucky to have jobs created by the city, mostly construction. They only made about 60% of what the non-welfare workers got, but it kept food on the table, and they learned a trade.

As a schoolboy, before the Depression, Al had wanted to become a doctor. Being relatively new immigrants, their father lost his factory job and all of their meager savings after the crash of '29. After three years of dire poverty and depression, their father, whether out of frustration or perhaps of embarrassment for not being able to provide for his family, did what many men in his situation did; one day he just left, never to return. During the Depression, this was sometimes called, *the poor man's divorce*. The young men had to drop out of school. Now a single mother, their Ma was able to apply for city welfare, *Aid to Women and Children*.

After several years of courting, and the end of the Depression in sight, Al finally landed a "real" job, at an electrical factory, and asked Gladys to be his bride. Harry and Blanche were also engaged, and in the wedding party. Emilia made the trip to Milwaukee for the wedding, and left Jan with Stan and Genja, as he was by now, too confused to travel. Ben gave the bride away. Mrs. Wehr not only had her seamstress make Gladys' exquisite gown and veil, she also gave them money for a modest wedding reception at the Polish Union Hall.

Gladys and Al moved in with Al's mother, Marion, to help her financially, and to save up for their own place. Luckily the apartment building was on the Lower East Side, and just a short trolley ride north along the lakeshore to the Wehr's. Harry and Blanche would soon join them, and the foursome, along with Marion and Al's younger sister, Teresa, rode out the end of the Great Depression in the tiny flat.

Toward the end of the Depression, dances and social gatherings became more prevalent. It was at one of these dances, at the Polish Club in near-by Wausau, that chance changed lives. Ben and his younger brother, Val, had driven with some friends from St. Casmir's.

The band was good, and played many popular tunes, not just the traditional polkas. Ben had seen a lady on the dance floor who seemed to really be enjoying the spirited music as much as he was, so he approached her and asked for the next dance. She seemed a bit flustered, and replied, "I think I am too old for you dear, but come meet my daughter!" Sitting off to the side, against a wall, was indeed, a much younger version of his intended dance partner. He introduced himself as Ben, to which she replied, "Irene". For the rest of the evening, 𝕿𝖍𝖊 𝕽𝖊𝖉 𝖅 seemed a million miles away. Irene, although young, was lovely, light on her feet, witty and self-assured. By the end of the night, they had promised to write to each other, and arrange to meet again. Ben did not know what to make of this new feeling. He had assumed that he would be a life-long bachelor, held hostage by 𝕿𝖍𝖊 𝕽𝖊𝖉 𝖅. Could this be the love of films and song? Ben did not realize until that evening, how terribly lonely he had been these past years, and how the toll of Jan's illness, and the trials of The Great Depression had reduced him to a squalid emotional state.

Irene Grych was also the child of Polish immigrants. Her parents, too, had a dairy farm between Stevens Crossing and Wausau. Unlike the large Zalewski clan, Irene had just two siblings, an older brother and sister, both married. Irene's sister and her family, like Joe and Josie, had moved to Chicago shortly after the Depression began, to find employment. She received a letter from Ben just a few days after their first meeting. He had asked her if she were going to attend the county fair in Wausau at the end of the month. Irene noticed that his English grammar was not the best, but she was so taken by his rugged movie star appearance, that she didn't care.

They met at the entrance to the fair a few weeks later. The Zalewski's had entered one of their prized Holsteins. Emilia had also entered a jar of her wild blueberry jam, and an arrangement of her most beautiful annuals. Wendy entered a flour-sack dress she had made in the latest fashion, complete with matching hat. Emilia had helped her dye the fabric with onion skins, and embroider the lapels and pockets. The entire family was in attendance, as were the Grych's, and most of the county. This was a much-anticipated annual event, and a welcome break from Depression woes. Emilia even brought Jan, praying to the Madonna that he *behave* and not throw a tantrum. These days, he was both docile and somewhat incoherent, or a raving madman.

Later in the afternoon, Ben met up with his family and introduced them to Irene and the Grychs. Emilia and Mary, Irene's mother, got on famously and each showed off their prize winning ribbons. Ben was thrilled to see Emilia smiling and happy. These past years had been hellish for her, too. Val was pleased with his red ribbon Holstein, and Wendy was awarded a blue ribbon for her flour sack ensemble! Ben was proud of Irene's three blue ribbons for her fruit pies. All-in-all, a great day; one all their souls and spirits needed.

All the Zalewski's noticed a change in Ben's demeanor. Emilia knew when she saw him with Irene that this was an answer to a prayer. Every mother wants their children to be happy. It hurt her to see Ben so unhappy for so long. He was such a hard worker, but so unlike his siblings in the fact that he was inquisitive, and seemed to see the inherent beauty of things, whether natural or man-made. She knew in her heart he was not a farmer, but had the soul of an artist. Between the role of eldest son, the Depression, and Jan's illness, unfortunately, this was his fate. It gave her great joy when Ben announced the following year that he and Irene were to be married.

JAN AND EMILIA

Jan's health appeared to be declining. Although his appetite was good, he had a hard time holding and using eating utensils. Emilia was content to let him use his fingers, and drink through a straw. He had also developed a palsy in his hands, and began to shuffle when he walked. He kept more and more to his favorite chair, and spent most days napping and paging through old seed, flower and machinery catalogs, as if seeing them for the first time. It broke Emilia's heart to see her strong and courageous husband failing in this way. He was now in his mid-sixty's, his hair still dark and wavy, but his eyes appeared as if a light had gone out from within. Ben and Emilia did not have to wait for the local doctor to diagnose him. It was clearly dementia made worse by Parkinson's disease.

Emilia was determined to care for Jan as long as she could, but when he became incontinent, and awoke at all hours of the night and wandered, he became a danger to himself and the rest of the family. She would often find him trying to dress at 4 am, and when she asked him why, he replied, "It's time for church." Sometimes Jan would follow at her heels all day, even when she had to relieve herself! If she were in the garden weeding, he often pulled the vegetable plants, instead. Emilia prayed to the Madonna daily. Daily prayers were so ingrained in Jan, that he still remembered the words to the rosary litany, although another family member had to begin to recite it. Gradually, he began to talk less and cry more. When he did talk, it was with harsh, angry and often foul language, usually accusatory. He seemed to know Emilia and Stan, although perhaps not their relationship. The children were as strangers to him.

As Emilia was making preparations for Ben and Irene's wedding, Jan snapped, and destroyed the lovely wedding cake, sending it flying across the kitchen floor. Luckily the girls were back at 𝕿𝖍𝖊 𝕽𝖊𝖉 𝖅 for the wedding, and could help. Needless to say, they were shocked by their father's deterioration since they had last seen him. Emilia tried to keep his condition low key in her letters so as not to worry them. This was the breaking point. Emilia burst into a fit of uncontrollable sobbing. She could not stop. One can only handle so much stress, even a rock like Emilia; the Depression, the never-ending list of chores, desperately missing her children and grandchildren, and feeling guilty hiding Jan's illness from them, constantly watching over a child-like spouse, trying to ignore his offensive and hurtful rantings, preparing for her son's wedding. By now, both spouses were weeping, and the Zalewski siblings were at a loss as to what to do. They had never seen these super-humans enervated like this.

After Ma calmed down, Bernice put her to bed with tea and brandy, and surprisingly, Emilia acquiesced. Ben set Pa in his chair, also with brandy, minus the tea. He put the rest of the bottle and several glasses on the large farmhouse table, and gathered his sibling and their spouses, most of whom had come for the impending wedding. Wendy, still young, had been terrified by what she had witnessed, and insisted on laying down next to Ma. Ben informed them about Pa's condition, and why Ma had tried to keep it from them. They all had their own crosses during these trying years. It was decided among them, that after Ben's honeymoon, he would have Pa placed in the County asylum in Wausau. He knew Emilia would not easily admit defeat, but they all worried about her health and stability, as well as Jan's safety. He would speak with Father Suleck after the wedding, and seek his counsel in dealing with Ma. She would listen to him. Unfortunately, this would not be a new problem for the good priest, as the asylum was crowded with unfortunate souls whose minds were lost to the Depression.

Uncle Stan promised to keep a steady eye on Jan at the wedding. The girls had remade a lovely wedding cake, and Josie and Bernice fried platters of chruscki and sugar dusted rosettes for the groom's dessert table. Irene and her mother made their famous pies, along with huge bowls of chicken soup with kluski, and trays of fried chicken and kielbasa, fresh picked green beans and sweet corn and plates of red ripe tomatoes and pickles. Gladys, ever the fashion plate, looked lovely in her yellow bridesmaid's dress, as did Wendy in mint green. Many of the parish were able to drive to Irene's church, St. Adalbert's, and after, to the Grych's farm for the reception. Everyone seemed so pleased that the handsome and talented Ben had found himself a wife. It was a glorious day. The entire area was happy to have something to celebrate. Emilia was so happy to have her offspring near again. Stan took care to see that Jan behaved. The blackberry schnapps helped. Many of the neighbors and parishioners had not seen Jan in a while, and could not help but be shocked by his demeanor. There had been local gossip, of course, as Jan had not been seen in church for some time.

Jack and Bernice were nice enough to drive the newlyweds back to Chicago with them, so they could honeymoon there. It was a long, hot ride, with their nephew Norbert wedged in with them. But they were "in love", so what did it matter? Ben could not wait to show his new bride his favorite places in the Windy City. Although Irene was attentive, she did not share the same excitement he had for the shops, theaters and museums, but rather, enjoyed walks along the great lake, riding *the El* or strolls down the grand avenues. He felt badly that he did not have more money to spend to really show her the sights, but few did at this time, and she said she was happy just to be away with him, secretly giddy to be seen walking on the arm of this handsome man, in her newly made honeymoon dress. They tried to visit Helena at the convent, but were told she was on retreat. Rules for visiting at the convent were very strict. After spending four glorious days taking in the sights, and unglamorous but tender nights in the Glowacki basement rooms, they boarded a train back to Stevens Crossing. As they passed through

Milwaukee, Ben began to feel anxious about the job ahead. He would have to take Pa to the County home. Thank God Uncle Stan, Fritz and Val would be there to help. Fr. Suleck had been making the arrangements while the newlyweds were gone. Irene noticed the sudden sadness, and with one look, alleviated his fears. It said she would always be his mainstay. And she was.

Jan was surprisingly compliant on the drive to the county seat. Emilia had tears in her eyes and could hardly speak. Ben and Fritz drove, with Fr. Suleck, whom they picked up at the rectory, in front with them. Little was said on the journey.

The facility itself, appeared to be clean and well-kept. Many patients, some in wheel chairs, were roaming the supervised grounds. Emilia was nauseous, clinging to her rosary beads. The good priest whom she trusted assured her that this was best, but her sense of loss and failure could not be assuaged. The boys led Jan to a large room, where he was shown his bed. The asylum was so crowded with men, that private rooms were only available to those who could manage to pay something. The wealthy were in fancier, private institutions. Many sounds could be heard from other areas of the building, including muffled shouts and screams. This made Emilia's blood run cold. Ben placed Jan's small collection of personal effects on the small table next to his assigned bed. Nothing sharp or pointed was allowed. His oldest son placed a small book of photographs, his beloved seed and flower catalogs, a wood carving he made his father of the Madonna, and his rosary beads. Jan immediately picked up the catalog and slowly began turning the pages with his palsied hands as he settled into the chair placed to the side of his bed. He did not even turn his head when the troupe left. Emilia, with tears streaming down her face, met with the doctor on duty who assured her they would do all they could to keep him safe and calm. For the time being, he would be in a ward with other men suffering a similar fate. Should he become worse, or violent, he may need to be drugged and/or restrained. Visitors were allowed on Sunday afternoons. Because the Zalewski's did not have telephone service, the doctor assured them they would receive a written report by mail weekly. The last thing Emilia remembered hearing as she left the ward to head back to the farm was the miserable cry, "Viola"!

OUT OF THE FRYING PAN, INTO THE FIRE

America was easing its way out of the Depression toward the end of the 1930's. Crop production had picked up a bit, and dairy prices rose slightly. With Pa away, the majority of the day-to-day challenges of running a farm were Ben's responsibility. Fritz, still bearing the pains of his automobile accident, never complained, unless Val got to the last sausage before he did at supper. He and Val were still living at home, and were an enormous help. Wendy was the only girl left at home, and helped Emilia and Ben's wife, Irene, around the house with the cooking and washing, not to mention the egg gathering, animal feeding, weeding and crop picking. The women were tough and not complainers, but Wendy could see the lack of light in her mother's eyes. Every Sunday after Mass, she had Fritz drive her to see Jan. He seemed to decline quickly after he left 𝕿𝖍𝖊 𝕽𝖊𝖉 𝖅. Eventually, he did not seem to recognize Emilia or the children. Every so often he would utter, "Viola", which broke Emilia's heart.

Irene and Ben had their first child in 1938. This was thrilling for the still young Wendy, who adored the sweet baby girl like a little mother. Lawrence had finished his schooling, and had gotten a job teaching at a local elementary school. Emilia was the proud mama at his graduation from the State Teacher's College in Stevens Crossing.

One of Lawrence's fellow students during his college years was Harold Szatko. Harold had proposed to his girlfriend upon graduation, and had asked Lawrence to be in the wedding party. He had also offered to put up the money for the white tuxedo, knowing Lawrence could not afford it. This was the first such formal affair for Lawrence, and he had to admit he looked rather debonair in the mirror being fitted for his wedding clothes. In the church processional, he was paired up with the bride's cousin, Genevieve Kurzynski. *Gene* as she was called, had shoulder-length, wavy dark brown hair, and large brown eyes to match. She was striking in her lime green chiffon bridesmaid dress and cascading floral headpiece. Lawrence was "gob smacked". He had little time nor money to date these past years.

He had spoken of course to a few girls in his classes, and was tempted to ask them out, but his confidence was shaken by his lack of money, his shabby albeit clean dress, but more importantly, his lack of time. When he wasn't studying, he was needed on the farm. He even looked for odd jobs around campus to earn a few extra cents, but during the Depression, even these were few and far between.

Perhaps because he was now a college graduate with a teaching post in a nearby town, or perhaps it was the free-flowing beer or the white tuxedo that gave Lawrence the confidence to ask the lovely Gene to dance at the wedding reception. In later years, he recalled it as one of the best days of his life. He and Gene would marry in 1938, and set up housekeeping in modest rented home with a wrap-around front porch on the main street of a small, nearby town where he was the elementary school teacher, grades 5 through 8.

When Chip was released from his three year duty at the CC camps, he headed to Chicago, and stayed with Bernice and Jack until he found a job as a gas station attendant. The owner was getting up in years and took a liking to Chip and admired his work ethic and knowledge of automobiles. Eventually, he became the station mechanic, and when the old man retired a few years later, he made Chip manager. With his dashing smile and Gablesque mustache, he got a lot of looks from the girls. He went out to a few church dances with Bernice and Jack, or stopped at the local tavern for a drink after work, but for the most part, he tried to save every penny hoping to buy the station from the old man. He wasn't even yet 20. His nephews Henry and Georgie Milewski and Norbie Glowacki were almost his age. They were always after him to go out. He was determined to get his shop before he thought about a wife and family.

Because Jack Glowacki worked for Illinois Bell Company, they had the luxury of a home telephone, paid for by the company for all its employees. On a cold, rainy March afternoon, Bernice was startled by the still unfamiliar telephone ring. It was Ben calling from the State Asylum informing her that Pa had passed during the night. The deterioration of his brain caused his bodily organs to shut down one by one. The doctors had told Emelia that the end was near at her last visit. She had Father Suleck come after Mass that Sunday to perform Last Rites. Wendy, Irene, Gene and the boys were present for the ceremony, as were Uncle Stan and his wife.

It was a tearful reunion at 𝕿𝖍𝖊 𝕽𝖊𝖉 𝖅. Even Sister Philothea was given permission to attend her father's funeral. She rode with the Milewski's from her post in Chicago, while Chip made his first trip back to the farm since leaving over five years earlier, riding with the Glowacki's. Al and Gladys came in a borrowed car from Milwaukee. Ben embraced his little brother, and tears flowed, but no words were ever again spoken about the incident that caused Chip to flee his home and family years earlier. Chip was introduced to his two new sisters-in-law, Irene and Gene, and newest nephew Freddie. He was shocked to see how his little sister, Wendy, had grown, and at sixteen, a beauty. She was so thrilled to see her much adored big brother, and would not let him out of her sight.

Chip longed to talk with his closest-in-age brother, Val. After all had gone to bed, the two brothers shared news of the past five years. The older confessed jealousy over the fact that his little brother had escaped farm life, and been able to see more of the world outside of Steven's Crossing. The younger spoke of his having nothing, including shoes to his name when he entered the CC Camp, and how difficult it had been to leave everything and everyone he loved behind, especially Ma. Val told Chip how much Ma and Pa appreciated the CC checks that came monthly from him and Fritz. Their sacrifice and hard work made it possible for the family to better survive the Depression. When Pa was sent to the asylum, Val felt more pressure than ever to remain on the farm to help Ben and Fritz. But now, with Pa gone, the shades of the Depression lifted, and Ben married with a family, he was planning on leaving 𝕿𝖍𝖊 𝕽𝖊𝖉 𝖅. He wanted to fly. As the first rays of sunrise were visible, Chip talked Val into coming to Chicago, and helping him run the station. He could perhaps save up for flying lessons.

The joy of seeing her children and grandchildren again, especially Chip and Helena (Sr. Philothea), who had been absent for so many years, brought some measure of comfort to Emelia's broken heart.

Jan was buried in the church graveyard next to his infant daughter who had passed so many years before. Perhaps it was good he did not live to see the pain brought by next year, 1941, when his sons and grandsons would be sent to War.

THE WAR YEARS

Everyone of this generation remembers where they were at a particular time in their lives, when they heard startling or tragic news. On Sunday, December 7th, 1941, most of the Zalewski clan had just returned from Mass at their respective churches. The Milewski and Glowacki families had gathered at Jack and Bernice's for Sunday dinner. They had also invited Chip, and Val who had recently joined him at the service station. Gladys was enjoying her one day off, playing pinochle with Al and his family. Fritz had met Jean after Mass and was going to take her out for coffee and a sandwich. Irene, Wendy and Emilia had just finished putting away the last of the dishes from a delicious venison dinner, thanks to Ben's fine hunting. Lawrence was grading math papers at his kitchen table. Sr. Philothea was filling out some paperwork to be admitted to teacher's college.

Without modern mass communication, word of the surprise Japanese attack on Pearl Harbor earlier that fateful morning, spread by telegraph and later radio to the mainland. Those with radios ran to inform their neighbors without. The blood of the men boiled, with a "let's get 'em" spirit, while the hearts of the women broke in anticipation of what this meant, the loss of husbands and sons to the dreadfulness of war.

Emilia had stopped receiving letters from her family still in Poland, after 1939, when Hitler had invaded the country. She had heard and read the horror stories of what the Nazi's had inflicted on her homeland. Daily prayers were offered up for those inhabitants, living and dead, both at home and by the Parish. It had been over two years since she heard anything.

Emilia had written her sister in Sulwaki that Jan had passed, not knowing if the communication ever reached her. Was Sulwaki still there, or did the Germans destroy it in their madness? The Polish language newspaper had news from abroad, but she had heard that much was censored by the Reich. It made her blood run cold to think of her family left at their mercy, and how easily she could still be among them. Now, with the advent of the war here in the States, would her fate, and that of her beloved family be any different?

The draft had been initiated the previous year with the possibility of war on the horizon. As much as the President wanted to stay out of it, he felt the need to prepare for the worst. All males 21-65 had to register. When war was finally declared after Pearl Harbor, the age requirements were changed; males 18-45 were now eligible for the draft. Ben, at 41, was considered III-A, because his mother was a widow, he was still supporting his sister as well as his own family, and because farming was necessary to the war effort. Fritz also received an IV-F deferment due to the injuries he sustained in the car accident. Education was considered necessary to the Homefront, therefore Lawrence was also deferred. Chip and his nephews, Norb, Henry and Georgie were eligible and waiting their turn to be called up.

Many men and boys did not wait to be drafted, but were gung-ho to "stick it to the Japs", after witnessing the devastating newsreels of the naval attack in Hawaii. Val, was one of them. Maybe this was his chance to fly! He was not altogether unhappy working with Chip at the filling station, but the garage was Chip's dream, not Val's, so he enlisted in the Army/Air Corps the week after Christmas, 1942, and was immediately off to basic training at Camp McCoy near Madison.

Because of the Japanese attack on the Pacific fleet, and its proximity to the American West Coast, defending the Pacific Northwest was prioritized. Its vulnerable shoreline made an easy target for enemy landing. When Val found out they were only taking officers, or high school graduates at the least for pilot training, he was devastated. But because of his interest in aviation, he was assigned to Fort Warden, Washington, a strategic defense port on the Olympic peninsula. It was a joint base for the Army, Navy and Coast Guard. His unit performed all manner of duty including clearing roads, paving runways, constructing telephone lines, and establishing radar and Aircraft Warning Systems. When he wasn't on duty or too dead tired, he would hike, and fish the area in awe of what God had created there. He had never seen a real snow-capped mountain, or caught a salmon. His letters to Emilia were filled with descriptions of the natural beauty of the state. Val made lots of friends among the other homesick draftees, sharing stories of their home states and hometowns. Many had girlfriends or wives and families. He was glad he did not have that responsibility and enjoyed his adventure so different from the farm life he knew.

Chip was called up early in 1943. He was more than willing to do his part for the war effort, but hated leaving the business he was trying to build. The fatherly owner promised not to retire until Chip returned, and said his old job would be waiting for him when the war ended.

Because of his background in auto mechanics, he was assigned to the motor pool, where he kept the necessary jeeps, transport trucks and tanks at the ready. His Marine unit was assigned to North Africa, where the heat and blowing sand made everyone's job harder. He was a long way from the flat prairies of Wisconsin. Thankfully, he was able to stay out of combat, but their location was attacked by enemy aircraft on more than one occasion. He was grateful to be spared, when so many of his fellow soldiers were not. Being a true child of the Great Depression, Private Zalewski let nothing go to waste; not one bolt nor electrical wire. His buddies referred to him as "the junk man". In fact, once when he came across some worn parachutes, he asked the quartermaster if he could have them. This parachute silk would later make its way to Emilia, and become the fabric of Wendy's wedding dress, Wendy's daughter's christening dress, and her great-granddaughter's christening dress, fifty years later.

Norb Glowacki was also called up in 1943 as were his cousins, Georgie and Henry Milewski. Norb opted for the Navy, the others, the Army. Henry, having completed two years at City College in Chicago, was sent to officer's training. He spent most of the War stateside near Washington, D.C., as a General's Aide. Georgie, like Norb, fought in the South Pacific, both fortunate to escape physically unscathed.

Gladys kissed her handsome soldier Al goodbye in 1942, tears streaming as he boarded a train to Texas where he would train as a medic. Maybe he would never be a doctor, but he vowed to learn all he could as a medic. Unfortunately, the battlefields of France, took their toll. He may have escaped with his life, but would never escape the bloody memories and nightmares that haunted him, for decades after his return. What he witnessed during the War would alter him for the rest of his life, and he would return to Gladys a changed man.

Fate intervened when Val had an errand to run at base headquarters. Mind elsewhere, he quite literally ran into someone, who dropped a huge stack of papers that flew everywhere. His first thought was, please don't let it be an officer! After profuse apologies, he bent down to help gather the scattered papers, and came face-to-face with an angel. Not a real angel mind you, but a sweet faced girl, with large blue eyes, heart-shaped red lips, and light sandy waves of hair. He was dumb-struck. When the papers had been gathered, the act of contrition continued, his explanations sounding to him like nonsense. The poor girl was blushing. Perhaps she was embarrassed for him. He somehow had the presence of mind to offer to buy her a soda at the PX to make it up to her. She said she could not leave her post except at lunch. Val took this rejection to assume she was either really mad, had a boyfriend, or just didn't want to be bothered.

After his errand was complete, he left by the rear exit to avoid another encounter with this young woman. He had known a few local Wisconsin girls back home that he'd met at church or at dances. He had a set his sights on the pretty Annie Chula, the daughter of the local tavern owner. The tavern had the only telephone for miles, so Val often made excuses to visit the tap on the premise of checking for news or messages, secretly hoping to see and flirt with Annie. He often dreamt of asking her out to the movies or for a soda, but the depression left little time or money for dating. Ben would never allow it. Still, he never forgot his first love interest, and in fact, forty years later Val returned to Stevens Crossing, looked her up and took her out, resulting in a short steamy two week affair.

Chip and his Chicago nephews had introduced him to some girls too, but he was too happy experiencing life to get serious about anyone. And then there was the War. There was something about this girl that haunted him, however. He couldn't get her face out of his thoughts. Similar to his early tactics pursuing Annie, he volunteered to run any and all errands that would take him to the headquarters building hoping to catch a glimpse of her, and maybe find out her name. Luckily, about a month later, he slid onto a stool at the PX to grab a soda, and there she was in a sapphire blue blouse, across the counter having her lunch. After he caught her eye, he ordered another soda, and had the waitress deliver it to her. She then caught his attention and lifted the glass as in a toast. When she got up to leave, Val, unsure what to do next, was relieved to see her coming toward him. She thanked him for the soda, and laughed about the minor catastrophe that had brought them together. The angel-face confessed that all the other office gals had teased her unmercifully. They formally introduced one another, as Val walked her back to headquarters. Her name was Joyce, and she was born and raised in the area, trying to do her part for the War effort. Val told her how mesmerized he was with the Pacific Northwest, and by the time they reached their destination, Joyce had promised to take him salmon fishing on Sunday afternoon. Heaven.

After that Sunday, they met whenever they could both get the time off. If was clear they were both smitten with one another. Although just twenty, he could hardly believe this gorgeous gal was still unattached. She thought him the most ruggedly handsome man she had ever seen. Joyce confessed she had been serious with a boy she had dated as a teen, but after he had to drop out of high school during the Depression to help out at home, they saw little of each other. Last she heard he was fighting in the Pacific.

About two months into their relationship, Val knew this was "the real thing"; the stuff of movies and love songs. He lived for their short times together. For those few hours the War seemed far removed from his thoughts. Luckily, because he was stateside, mail from home came regularly. He was thrilled to hear that Lawrence and Gene had welcomed a son, and that his brother Chip, and Gladys's husband, Al, were both safe despite being in harm's way overseas. Enlisted nephews were alright as well. Norb had written of a serious Japanese attack to his ship, and how proud he was that the destroyer's anti-aircraft guns brought down two Jap planes. He could just imagine Emilia on her beads to the Madonna at least twice a day praying for their safety. Val felt fortunate to be where he was, and stopped complaining when he was woken from sleep by piercing air raid sirens.

As much as he adored Joyce, Val felt he could not ask for her hand until the War was over. There was always the chance for him to be deployed overseas, or perhaps invasion by Japanese forces. On one of their rare Sundays together, Joyce took him to her father's cabin on the Sound to fish, and check his Dungeness crab pots. After an hour or so, the wind picked up, and the rain began in earnest. Nothing new for this part of the state, but they ran for shelter to the cabin. Both were soaked, so Val lit a fire, and they huddled near to dry off and get warm, sharing a blanket draped over their shoulders. She was not like the floosy Chicago girls he'd met, or the shy Annie from Wisconsin, but she seemed classier somehow; more mature. They could not help themselves. The pressures of the time in which they lived temporarily melted away as they found tenderness and passion in each other's arms.

Lost in love, Val was almost AWOL getting back to post. It would have been worth a week in the stockade.

Unfortunately, a few weeks later, Val was sent to Fort Lewis, near Tacoma, over eighty miles away. It was to be an eight week anti-aircraft training class. He was thrilled to be chosen for the assignment as it meant being around the fighter planes at the airfield there, however, it also meant being away from Joyce for two months. Luckily he was kept busy with his classes and duties at Fort Lewis, and even met another private there from Stevens Crossing. Their friendship helped the weeks pass.

When at last he returned to Ft. Worden, before reporting for his assignment, he went to see Joyce at the headquarters building. He knew they would not have time to talk, but he wanted her to know he was back, and arrange a date. She had a sheepish look on her face when she saw him, not quite what he had expected. Perhaps she was embarrassed that he visited her at work, or this would get her into trouble with her supervising officer. Without smiling, she slipped him a note and asked him to meet her outside the PX at retreat. The day crawled by. His mind raced. Did she find someone else while he was gone? When the bugler finally sounded retreat, and his replacement showed, he raced from his radar post, hoping she had waited for him. And there she was. His beautiful Joyce, tears streaming down her lovely cheeks. He held her close and could feel her legs weaken as she leaned against him. Val led her to a nearby bench under a large pine tree, somewhat secluded from prying eyes. It all came flooding out of her amid tears and sobs. Yes, she still loved him with all her heart, but she was pregnant and scared to death. His life flashed before him in an instant.

They were married in the Post chapel in a small ceremony a week later. Joyce looked lovely in her rose colored wedding suit and white orchid corsage. It was not the way either of them had envisioned, but they were in love, and it was wartime. Maybe it was a good thing Pa was gone, as he wouldn't understand. His new bride's father was less-than-pleased, and made no secret about his feelings to Val. Emilia would be shocked at first to learn he'd taken a wife, especially a young, Protestant one. With the world in chaos, he hoped she would try to understand. He enclosed a wedding photo of the two of them in his letter to Ma. They made a dashing couple especially with Val in uniform (with corporals' stripes).

In spring of 1945, Lilian Milewski announced to Joe and Josie that she was going to enter the order of the Sacred Heart Sisters, following in the footsteps of her beloved aunt Helena. So far her two brothers, Henry and Georgie had survived the War, and were both stateside. Although Josie was sad to see her only daughter leave home, she was proud of the choice she had made, and knew the sweet girl would make a wonderful nun. Helena, now Sr. Philothea, was there at the motherhouse in Chicago for Lilian's commitment ceremony, beaming. They had become close these past couple years, as Lilian sought her council on joining the novitiate. Sr. "Phil" had just returned from teacher's college in Wisconsin, where she received a degree in English with a minor in Home Economics. Emilia was proud. Before she had met Jan, she had thought that she, too, might become a nun. It seemed a million years ago. It also frightened her to think of what that might have entailed had she stayed in Poland. The stories that she heard about how the religious were treated by the Germans and Russians were terrifying.

In 1942, Wendy was encouraged by Gladys to come to Milwaukee. She was lonely with Al at War, and she knew from Wendy's letters that she felt like a bit of a "fifth wheel" living with Ben, Irene, their two young children, and Ma. So armed with the few dollars she had saved from cleaning part-time at the funeral home in Steven's Crossing, and the money Gladys had sent for train fare, she left 𝕿𝖍𝖊 𝕽𝖊𝖉 𝖅 to join her sister. Gladys had gotten her a job in a dress shop as a seamstress. One of her co-workers there introduced Wendy to her cousin, Tomek, a young polish boy, who was immediately taken with Wendy's auburn hair and green eyes. Because Gladys was so much older, she put strict curfew rules on her. She was also worried that Wendy was perhaps naive when it came to dating, having spent most of her young life isolated on the farm. She allowed Tomek to take Wendy to the movies and supervised parish dances. As happened to many young courtships these days, the War intervened and Tomek was called up to serve. Wendy promised to write, and even gave him her picture to carry. Now she joined her sister every night to pray the rosary for their soldiers.

Miraculously, the Zalewski clan, and their extended families, survived the War, although some better than others. Unfortunately, Wendy was notified that Tomek had been killed in France. She was understandably devastated, as was his cousin Anna at the dress shop. The two of them joined the ranks of those there who mourned.

Army Specialist "Doc" Al Rogalinski came home in 1945 a changed man. He was incredibly thin, and suffered from traumatic nightmares. Poor Gladys felt helpless. Even her incredible cooking could not fatten him up or lift his spirits. Wendy had moved in with her friend, Jeanette, from the shop for a few months, to give Gladys and Al some much needed time alone together.

As a combat medic on the battlefields of France, he could not un-see the horrors of war, the mutilated bodies, pain of body and soul, the cries and pleading from the dying. These were just boys, like him, from the farms, fields, towns and cities of every inch of America. How many pair of eyes did he have to close, how many promises did he have to make to dying soldiers to tell their loved ones good bye? The once sacred and beautiful stone churches of rural France, now bombed-out-makeshift hospitals, where dusty pews served as cots and altars as operating tables. Engraved memories of a fellow medic sprinting across a battlefield to save a fallen soldier only to be shot by the Germans, having used the fallen as bait to pick off yet another American, paying no heed to the red cross on his helmet. Once peaceful meadows littered with human remains.

His letters and postcards home were few and far between, but when they arrived, they had been upbeat and full of stories of his French experience, especially the liberation of Paris. In fact, he brought home several Parisian souvenirs for his bride, and his mother. Gladys was completely unprepared for the effect the war would have on her young husband for the rest of their lives. The heavy drinking was at first expected, celebrating the return of the troops and the end of the war in Europe. But, it became a daily routine. Most of those first months following his return, were spent fitfully sleeping until noon and then gulping cup upon cup of black coffee nursing hangovers, until it all began again later in the day. He needed to find work, but Gladys did not want to pressure him, and she was still employed by the Wehrs. After a few months, she confided in his mother and sister-in-law. They both agreed that something had to be done. Blanche's husband, Harold, had also survived the war, and often joined Al in their binging. However, Harold did not make this a daily event as did his brother, and sought out employment after a few weeks home. The women pleaded with him to speak to Al about the excessive drinking, and perhaps help him find employment. Mr. Wehr had offered work at his steel plant, but it had fallen on deaf ears. It was as if Al were paralyzed, and could not cope with daily life. It was breaking Gladys' heart and her spirit. Sympathy was giving way to anger she could no longer control. She thought perhaps she may be pregnant by now, but due to his near constant stupor, this was not to be.

Harold suggested their parish priest talk to Al. He had always been a faithful Catholic man, and perhaps he would listen to clergy. Indeed, it seemed to help. Gladys invited the cleric to dinner a few times a month. Al seemed to "shape-up" when the priest came, and often had conversations with the man over coffee and cigarettes in the living room, while Gladys cleaned up after dinner. It helped that Fr. Zwick had been a chaplain during the war. He witnessed much of the same horror. They could share their trauma. Fr. Zwick helped Al find work at a local factory, where they were looking for a maintenance person, a jack-of-all-trades so to speak. The once aspiring doctor never wanted anything to do with medicine again, so he took the job, and stayed with that company until he retired thirty-five years later.

The kind priest was often a fixture at dinner, never refusing a meal from the best cook around. The drinking did not stop, but was somewhat curtailed, especially during the week. In his heart, Al wished only the best for Gladys, and hoped she could stop working, and raise a family. As more boys came home from the war, and victory was finally declared over Japan, Al's nightmares seemed to lessen a bit. Telling "war stories" with other vets seemed to help, although none of them relived the horrific parts, at least not out loud. It seemed it was all about Aces, Tanks, Pigalle, Parisian women, and exotic sounding liquors if you were in Europe, or Kamikazes', bare chested women and grass skirts if you were in the Pacific.

A year after Al returned, Gladys went to see a doctor, hoping she could find out why she was not yet a mother. She thought it might have been Al's drinking. The doctor explained that the emergency operation she had undergone at nineteen, involved her ovaries. She was so naïve at the time she did not understand the complications, but did remember Mrs. Wehr in tears after talking to the doctor following the procedure. The operation had left her sterile.

EMILIA, POST WAR

Emilia was now in her 60's, and a widow. She was tired. Irene had taken on much of the "woman's work" at the farm, except for the cooking and housekeeping which Emilia continued to do. The house was full. Ben and Irene now had two little ones. So when Irene's mother, Mary Grych, suggested Emilia move to Steven's Crossing, she did just that. Mary, herself now a widow, had sold their farm and bought a house in Steven's Crossing near one of her daughters. It was one block from St. Peter's Church, and close to the market. Emilia could rent the upstairs apartment for a modest amount. She had always gotten along well with Mary. It would be someone her own age to talk to and reminisce. They could walk to daily Mass, something Emilia was especially thankful for. She had many prayers of thanksgiving to offer up, as her boys all survived the War. Ben was willing to pay the reasonable rent, and after forty years, Emilia left her home, The Red Z, to begin a new stage of her life, living alone.

It was difficult at first to adjust to "the quiet". How do you cook for "one"? After a month or two, she and Mary had gotten into a routine of walking to morning Mass, unless there were blizzard-like conditions, and then sharing breakfast at one or the other's apartments. In the afternoons, they would putter in Mary's small garden, go to the local market or dry goods store, or play bunco. A few evenings a week she would go downstairs to listen to Mary's radio with her. On Fridays, they played pinochle in the church hall. Every Saturday Emilia baked bread and rolls for the week, that Ben would then take back to The Red Z for Irene when he stopped to see her after Mass. The children were especially delighted when *Busia* included sweets like paczki or chruscki. Pies were still Irene's specialty, however.

Emilia still helped out at the farm, especially during harvest-time, when Irene had her hands full with the children, and trying to make three huge meals a day for the harvesters. Most of the farmers took turns harvesting their crops, borrowing each other's implements and manual labor. The farmer's wife traditionally provided meals for all the workers. Emilia and Mary were always willing to help during canning season and berry season, making all varieties of delicious preserves. As much as she loved seeing her grandchildren, and feeling useful and needed at *the Z*, it was always nice to come home to the quiet of her new city life with all its amenities, such as electricity and telephone service!

Emilia and Mary even took a couple trips together by train to see their relatives in Milwaukee and Chicago. It was nice to have a companion who also spoke better English than she did. Because she always insisted Polish be spoken in her home, she, herself, did not have the grasp of the English language that her children did, having learned at school.

In 1948, life was beginning to return to normal following the War Years. The farm was turning a nice profit, as young soldiers returned home, married and started families which created a demand for food and dairy. During the hay harvest of that year, Emilia and Mary were at the farm helping Irene with childcare and cooking to feed the harvesters. It was a hot, humid Indian summer day. The skies were ominous threatening rain. It was mid-afternoon and the women had just finished cleaning up after lunch and were preparing to begin the evening meal, when the skies opened up. Because of the lightning, most of the men took shelter in the barn. Irene saw the headlamps of a car coming up the drive from the main road, splashing through the muddy ruts. As it came closer, she recognized it as the Chula's, owners of the nearest local tavern, and telephone. She opened the door as she saw Mike Chula exit the car. She explained that Ben was in the barn, mid-harvest, and Chula took off in the direction of the barn before explaining what he had come for. After what seemed like seconds, she saw both men running back toward the house, soaking wet. Ben yelled, "Pack me a bag", "I'm going to change." Irene ran to their bedroom after him, and as he peeled off his soaking wet overalls, he told her that Chula's had gotten a call for them from Joe Milewski. Their eldest son, Georgie, Ben's godson, had drown at a lake during a company picnic near Chicago. Minutes later, Ben was dressed in his suit, Irene's change-of-clothes packed in his small valise. Meanwhile Emilia and Mary heard the horrible news from Mike Chula. Emilia grieved for her step-daughter, Josie. She had already suffered so much in her young life, and had been so relieved that her boys had survived the War! What cruel fate. Ben, giving no thought to the harvest, knew he had to be there for his closest sibling. Mike Chula agreed to take him to the train. Irene raided the empty flour canister for a few dollars she had saved there, shoved them in his pocket, and kissed him goodbye. The three women stood frozen in the kitchen with tear streamed faces, the two frightened children cried, as bolts of thunder and lightning shook the room.

By the time the storm had passed, it was near supper, and the harvesters, having heard the news, decided to head to their respective homes, and resume the harvest the next day. Irene had no time to grieve. She was in charge now, and their entire hay crop depended upon her ability to take charge. Thank goodness for Emilia and Mary doing child and kitchen duty! Losing one's self in hard work is one way to cope with loss, Emilia thought, although she worked on the verge of tears...tears for her daughter, her grandson and his siblings, and their father. They had come so far after losing the factory during the Depression. Georgie had landed himself a nice corporate job after the War, and was engaged to be married. Josie would never get over it. When Joe died of a massive heart attack a few years later, she became more and more despondent, in an eerie way, reminiscent of her father.

CHICAGO

After the War, Jack and Bernice's only child, Norbert, returned from the Navy. His uncle, Chip, had also recently returned from the conflict, and had gone back to the Chicago service station he had worked in before the War as a manager. As business picked up in the post-war years, the station was looking to hire another attendant/mechanic. The owner was now retired, and was allowing Chip to purchase the business from him, with his VA benefits. He talked his nephew Norb into taking the new position, eventually working the business into a partnership. This proved beneficial to them both, as Chip had an employee he could trust, and one who knew his stuff. Norb had learned a lot in his Navy years that forced him quickly from teenager to adult. Bernice was pleased to have her brother working with her son.

Bernice was very close to her sisters Helen and Josie. Helen (Sr. Philothea) was teaching English and Home Economics at a Catholic girl's school in Chicago. Georgie's death took a toll on them all. As Josie's depression worsened, Bernice and Sr. Phil made it their mission to visit as often as possible. Every few weeks, Bernice would take the bus cross town to Josie's, and then Joe or later, her son, Henry, would drive them to the convent near the school where Sr. Phil taught. Being the Home Economics teacher, they often met in Phil's classroom, where she managed to always have coffee and treats. On rare occasions when Jack or Henry would join them, she even managed to produce cold, bottled beer! (The stories of the miraculously appearing beer would always come up in later years when reminiscing about

Sr. Phil.) Josie missed her daughter, now Sr. Ernest Marie. Although they were of the same order, Ernest was assigned to an orphanage in Milwaukee. She managed to get to the Chicago motherhouse a couple times a year. Henry also drove Josie the ninety miles north to Wisconsin to see her when time and weather permitted.

Now that Emilia was "retired", she and Mary Grych took bus or train trips to see relatives in Milwaukee or Chicago. Rarely having left 𝕿𝖍𝖊 𝕽𝖊𝖉 𝖅, these were monumental experiences for Emilia, which she cherished. Bernice and Jack had a nice home on the South Side, in a predominantly Polish neighborhood with a third bedroom for Emilia to stay when she visited. Their Parish, St. Casmir's' also had a pastor of Polish descent, so homilies were in Polish and Mass in traditional Latin. Bernice loved taking her mother downtown on the bus, to show her the big city sights. It was here that Emilia saw her first motion picture. The theater took up the greater part of a city block, with a four story vertical sign in neon lights proclaiming, *Chicago.* The vast three thousand seat interior was as impressive as the outside, with its Baroque use of plush red and gold velvet, ornate lighting including sparkling crystal chandeliers, gold-toned exquisitely carved ornamentation, a magnificent staircase and painted murals. A huge Wurlitzer theater organ played before the film and newsreels started. It was the grandest thing Emilia had ever seen.

The newsreel that preceded the feature film, focused on the Post-War world, mainly in Europe, with the establishment of NATO, the rising spread of Soviet influence, and America's involvement in the Berlin airlift. How often Emilia wondered how her relatives still in Poland survived the German, then Soviet occupation. She had yet to get any correspondence from any of them. The rumors were enough to keep her awake some nights and on her knees most days in prayer.

"I Remember Mama", featuring Irene Dunne and Barbara Bel Geddes was the film they saw. Although Emilia's English was still not good, she understood more than she was able to speak. Bernice filled in the story line when needed, but the tender story of an immigrant mother's love, needed little interpretation. In a way, it was the story of her own life.

MILWAUKEE

few years after the War ended, Mr. Wehr died of a massive coronary. Mrs. Wehr decided to sell the lakeshore mansion and move in with her oldest son, who had taken over the reins of the business. He and his family also owned a large, formal house with a complete staff. The ever-loyal Mrs. Wehr said she would find a position for Gladys, but Gladys refused, knowing she could make more money, with less time away from home, working at the same factory as her husband. They could come and go together, and she could monitor what he did after work, which usually involved drinks at the corner tavern.

Because they both still wanted a family, adoption had been discussed. Gladys carefully filled out myriads of paperwork, and had gotten glowing references from the Wehrs, but when the woman from social services showed up at their apartment door around dinnertime for an impromptu interview, she found the house spotless, a delicious smelling dinner at the ready, but no sign of Al. Gladys tried to make excuses for his being late for dinner, and prayed he would not show up until the woman had gone. After fifteen minutes, the social worker rose to leave taking two of Gladys' homemade pastries with her to enjoy after dinner. Gladys felt a sigh of relief opening the door for her until she heard the sound of boots on the stairs. Al stumbled on the top step and landed spread-eagle at the foot of the startled woman. He reeked of beer, booze and cigarettes. His work clothes were dirty and oil-stained. Gladys helped him to his feet and inside the apartment. She tried all manner of excuses for her husband's demeanor, mainly "the War", but the social worker had seen this scenario many times before. Not the environment for a child. Gladys was inconsolable.

Wendy, still grieving after having lost her first beau to the War, continued on at the dress shop. She and friend, Jeanette, shared a small flat near the shop. They were both often welcome dinner guests at Gladys', where they unfortunately, witnessed many of Al's drunken episodes. Wendy's heart broke for her sister, who because of the age difference, was more like a mother to her. When sober, Al was the sweetest most attentive of men. He was handy around the house, and deeply loved his wife. Known at his job as a hard worker and problem solver, it was hard to see this personality change through alcohol. Movies, papers and magazines were full of stories of Post-War trauma among vets; Al was not alone in his retreat into the bottle. None-the-less, the families they returned to, were now also victims of war.

Ever frugal as raised, Gladys saved her pennies until she had enough saved to buy a two acre lot at the edge of town. The recently passed G I Bill, allowed them to acquire a loan to build a house at a reasonable rate. It was here on Mill Road, that Gladys and Al would almost single-handedly try to not only build a new home, but rebuild their life together. Plans for the building, and clearing of the lot took most of their free time, thus keeping Al from his seat at the local tavern, at least on weekends. Al's brother worked construction and served as the project foreman. It took the better part of three years to build and finance the two bedroom brick bungalow, but it gave them a common goal and sense of pride. The acreage allowed them to put in a huge vegetable and flower garden, after all, Gladys was a farm girl at heart.

Wendy's roommate, Jeanette Jersazk, had met a nice boy at a local church dance. He was recently discharged from the Army, having served in the Pacific. Currently, he was working a Civil Service job at the main Post Office in Milwaukee, hoping to become a letter carrier. Polish and Catholic, they had everything in common, and were soon a *couple*. Stan Werbinski could not help but like Jeanette's roommate. The green-eyed Wendy was pretty, talented and smart, and perfect, he thought, for one of his buddies at the Post Office, Bob Drews. Bob was lanky and tall, over six feet, with light blondish hair, blue eyes, and a great smile. He, too, had served in the Pacific, and had a mutilated thumb and small monthly stipend to show for it. The only problem Stan could see, was that he was of German descent, and worst of all, Lutheran. A double-date was arranged, and from that night on, it was the four of them. Stan and Jeanette were married first, Bob acting as Stan's Best Man, and Wendy as a bridesmaid. Bob proposed shortly thereafter. Gladys liked Bob, his tall good looks, and ambition. He was currently using his G. I. benefits to further his education in accounting taking night classes after work at the Post Office. What she didn't approve of, however, was his religion. He was raised a strict Lutheran, even attending parochial school. At this time, Catholics did not marry Protestants without some sense of scandal. Emilia would never understand. Bob's mother, also a widow, was equally distraught.

Life changed quickly in the United States after the War. GI's brought home *War brides,* many of whom were European, Australian or in some cases, Japanese. Many of these returning soldiers and sailors sought out work in the larger cities rather than returning to their small hometowns where their foreign brides might face prejudice or ridicule. So, too, taboos regarding differing religions were lessening, and easier to deal with in a large city like Milwaukee.

Bob, being a baptized Christian, agreed to let Wendy raise any children they might have as Catholics, although he refused to become a Catholic, himself (a "stubborn German", as Emilia would say). Gladys helped Wendy break the news to Emilia, who took it surprisingly well. Perhaps she was too tired to undergo the conflict that would ensue, or perhaps she was just happy to see her youngest child happy, and married to a good man. She prayed about it, and sought council from her Pastor and her daughter, Sr. Philothea, who assured her that God loved all his children, Catholic or Protestant

Gladys, of course as Matron-of-Honor put herself in charge of the wedding planning. She also threw her two wedding showers, one at 𝕿𝖍𝖊 𝕽𝖊𝖉 𝖅, so her mother, sisters-in-law and cousins could attend, and one in Milwaukee for the local relatives, and her friends at the dress shop. Even *Sr. Phil* and Cousin *Sr. Ernest Marie* came. Each, of course, was highlighted by Gladys' fabulous canapes, desserts and pastries on silver trays given to her by Mrs. Wehr. Wendy felt so special and loved. Bob's mother and aunts were even impressed! At the dress shop, Wendy had purchased a pattern in the latest style for her wedding gown. Emilia insisted on sewing the dress for her daughter using the parachute silk Chip had sent her from North Africa. Wendy was so thrilled that her mother did not try to stop her marriage to Bob that she readily acquiesced. The girls at the dress shop provided lace and material for her veil. Little did she know at the time that her granddaughter would wear this same veil on her wedding day almost eighty years later.

So, on a lovely Saturday in late May, Bob and Wendy were married in the rectory of Holy Family Parish, Fr. John Chula, presiding. Because Bob was Protestant, they could not be married inside the church proper. Stan and Gladys were their attendants/witnesses. Both Emilia Zalewski and Olga Drews were there, the city-born German-Lutheran and the Polish-Catholic farmer's wife, with a mixed entourage of family and friends enjoying the wedding dinner and dancing, good food and drink making friends of them all!

The newlyweds rented the upper half of a duplex, across from the County Zoo. Bob's brother, Chuck, his wife, Hazel, and their infant son lived downstairs. There were four Drews boys, Bob being the oldest. His father and mother were victims of a *Depression Divorce,* and Bob had not seen his father, Edward, since he inexplicably left when Bob was sixteen leaving him, the oldest, and responsible for the family. Olga insisted he stay in school, but the boys all pulled their weight selling papers on the street corner, sweeping storerooms, or anything else they could find to earn a few cents. He never forgot the lessons learned during those days, the value of hard work, and the importance of frugality. The three oldest boys were all very close in age and devoted to their mother and each other, all were veterans. The youngest, Allan, was still in high school, with plans on joining the Navy after graduation.

After about six months of marriage both Wendy and her sister-in-law, Hazel, found themselves pregnant. It was nice to have Hazel close, as the voice of experience. Thrilled with the news, she was terrified to tell Gladys, as she was afraid it would break her heart, knowing how badly she had wanted a baby of her own. Gladys put on a brave front, and was ever-the-proud-auntie. She and Al would dote on the child and her forthcoming brother, for the rest of their lives.

Hazel gave birth to another boy, the middle of May, 1948, and Wendy had a baby girl, just a few weeks later, shortly after celebrating her first wedding anniversary. She often related the story that Bob missed the birth as he was at his beloved Milwaukee Braves' baseball game when her child came into the world. Bob, ever the popular music aficionado, wanted to name her *Diane,* after a current song with that title. Wendy added *Marie,* a more *Catholic* appellation. Diane Marie spent at least two weekends a month on Mill Road with her *Atch* and *Unk* as she called them. They even bought her a dog to play with. Gladys taught her flowers-from-weeds in her garden and Al taught her to pick just the ripest berries and how to pull carrots.

Toward the end of the War, Fritz and his bride, Jean, moved to Milwaukee. The factories there were in need of workers to help churn out materials for the War effort. Women could fill some of these jobs, but many involved hard, physical labor. The summers in the factory were sweltering, and winters cold, but Fritz was no stranger to hard work, and with his brothers overseas fighting, he wanted to do his part for the War effort.

Jean, like her sister-in-law Gladys, had trouble conceiving. After several years of marriage, they, too, opted for adoption. Even though Fritz was *older* than the typical new father, he had a steady job, and owned a small bungalow. Near Christmas of 1949, after eight years of marriage, a newborn baby girl was placed with them. They were smitten with Patricia Anne.

When Diane was not yet two, Wendy and Gladys left Al to babysit, while they ran out shopping. Gladys had hidden any beer or liquor for fear he might be tempted to drink and not pay attention to the child. Frustrated when he could not find "a drop to drink", Al donned the child in her snowsuit and put her in the front seat of his Chevy, this being the era before car seats and seatbelts. His comrades at the local tavern were quite taken with the little girl, and she was more than happy on her uncle's lap at the bar, entertained with stir sticks, coasters, grape soda and popcorn. When she at last became bored and they both became soaked from her wet diapers, Al decided it was time to go. He knew his wife and sister-in-law would be furious when they saw the evidence of his misadventure. Luckily, he spotted a child's clothing store a few doors down from the tavern. Inside, a friendly, but skeptical sales clerk listened to Al's explanation. She was leery about helping until Al pulled several bills from his wallet. When they arrived home, little Diane was a fashion plate in a black, green and red plaid dress with white collar, matching red sweater and socks, and black patent leather shoes. The ladies did not know what to make of this upon their return. Luckily, Al was not falling down drunk. He was drinking coffee, grinning from ear to ear, and the adorable little girl seemed no worse for the wear. It was clear Al adored her and treated her like his own. The two women did not have the heart to sound off, but left the man with a calm but stern warning not to ever travel alone again with such a young child in the automobile. They both thanked St. Christopher for protecting this escapade!

Weekly card games on Mill Road became legendary, pinochle, poker, canasta or sheepshead. Fritz, Jean, Bob and Wendy were regulars, often joined by Stan and Jeanette, Al's brother and his wife, or one of Bob's brothers. The Rogalinski house on Mill Road had a mammoth dining room set, a *cast-off* Gladys had acquired from the Wehrs, with room enough for many players. Bob's specialty was making hi-balls, drinks popular at the time.

Al's drinking had subsided a bit, especially while they were occupied with house building, but the family social events unfortunately, encouraged it. The Milwaukee cousins, *Patsy* and Diane, became like sisters because their parents were together so often. They stayed at each other's houses, learned to play canasta and had their own card parties complete with kiddie cocktails made by one of their dads.

A couple times a year, the Drews' drove *up north* to visit Wendy's family in the Stevens Crossing area. Lawrence was still teaching in a small town outside of Stevens Crossing; he and Gene had suffered through several miscarriages and a still birth. Five of the children grew to adulthood. Three of them were close to Diane in age, and they became great pals. Diane loved the rural brand of fun such as catching pollywogs and fireflies, or swimming in one of the many area lakes. Her cousins, however, yearned for the city life with movies, ballgames and shops. The grass is always greener.

Ben and Irene had four children at 𝕿𝖍𝖊 𝕽𝖊𝖉 𝖅, the first a girl, Delores. Ben, always mesmerized with the cinema, named her after the sophisticated and glamorous film star Delores Del Rio, who was often termed, *the female Rudolph Valentino*. Some said she was the most beautiful woman to ever set foot in Hollywood. She was a miniature of her mother, Irene, with Ben's dark eyes. Two boys followed, Fred and Kenny, and then, after five years, another girl, Sally. She and Diane were almost the same age. Just like her other cousins, they believed city life to be magical; Diane thought jumping off the loft in the barn into mounds of hay, collecting eggs and playing with the animals, infinitely superior to anything Milwaukee had to offer. Just as she never saw all the labor involved in running a farm, her cousins didn't realize that movies and shops were mostly for the rich, which they were not. Living in a rented duplex, meant small rooms, small yards, crowded schools and streets, and crime.

The city was also a breeding ground for the disease, Poliomyelitis, a virus, which began with flu-like symptoms, could affect the central nervous system and cause paralysis, or even death. The virus seemed to affect mainly children during the hot, summer months. Mothers were warned not to let their children run and get overheated, or play in large groups. Many swimming pools and theaters in affected areas were closed. By 1952, over 57,000 cases were reported in the U.S., over 21,000 children paralyzed. Some children had to be placed in breathing chambers, called *iron lungs*, to help them breathe. The most famous polio victim and proponent of finding a cure was, of course, former President Franklin D. Roosevelt, who contracted the disease during an early epidemic around 1921. It left him paralyzed.

School children everywhere were given folders with twenty slots, each the size of a dime. Students were charged to fill each slot with the coin, and return them to their teachers. Some went door-to-door, others used their allowances, babysitting or paper route money. Relatives and friends were hit up for donations. These were sent to President Roosevelt's *March of Dimes* project to fund a cure for Polio.

Although there was no cure found, with this financial support, in the mid 1950's, a vaccine was developed by Dr. Jonas Salk and in the 1960's, an oral version of the vaccine was developed by Dr. Albert Sabin, a Polish-American that eradicated polio in the United States.

WASHINGTON

After the War, Val, Joyce and their son, Jeffrey, settled near Joyce's family home near Port Townsend. Val had fallen in love with the Pacific Northwest, and had no desire to return to the Midwest. He missed Ma and his siblings, however, especially Chip, being closest in age. Returning vets were marrying in droves and starting families creating the aptly named *baby boom*. With G I Bill benefits, they were looking to buy or build houses. Ever the entrepreneur and risk taker, Val decided he would start a construction business with a few G I buddies. Lumber was plentiful, and land was cheap. As project manager, he handled the accounts, ordering of supplies and the selling aspect of the business, while others did hands-on construction, land purchasing, loans and the like. It was lean going for the first few years, but soon the small business began to show profit.

He and Joyce had a lovely new home of their own in one of the new sub-divisions of Port Townsend. A shiny new Packard was in their garage. Val became a man-about-town. One of his new clients, the Rudzinski's, were, like him, Midwestern transplants who decided to settle here in Washington following the War. Sheila and Don decided on a lot in the new second phase of the sub-division. Theirs would be the first home built there. Val and Sheila spent a lot of time together walking the property, deciding on the home's placement, and later meeting to discuss finishes, colors, carpets and the like. Don rarely attended these meetings, busy with his current job as a chef and restauranteur, and trusting his wife to make these decisions. Don was like many vets, pouring his heart and soul into getting his business off the ground. He was away most evenings cooking and supervising the restaurant. When he wasn't in his office at work ordering or taking in supplies, he was sleeping.

Sheila was young, like Joyce, pretty and easy to talk to. She and Val found they had a lot in common with their Polish-Catholic Midwestern upbringing. Her parents, as well as Don's, were also immigrants, so they shared stories, laughs and sometimes tears remembering those who did not come home from the War, including Sheila's older brother, Davie, a Navy vet who died in the Pacific. Val found more and more excuses to be with Sheila, and she, being alone most of the time, also sought his company. Little did they realize, that Joyce was feeling the same loneliness with Val so wrapped up in his business, rarely home except to sleep.

The first time he kissed her was in the shadows framing her future house, facing the woods, where they had stopped to observe a doe with her fawn. She did not resist. They found more and more reasons to meet, both spouses seemingly oblivious to the situation. Late afternoons at the current Rudzinski residence were *safe* for them both; Don was at the restaurant, and Joyce home preparing the evening meal, not really expecting her husband until dinnertime. Val was often out of the office at building sites or meeting clients, so when he couldn't be reached by phone, she was not suspicious. Their Catholic guilt was overtaken by passion. Both still claimed to love their spouses, and made no plans to be permanently together. Joyce, however, noticed subtle changes in her husband. He began drinking more, especially during the week. He rarely touched her as he claimed to be too tired or too drunk. She knew how passionate he was about his business, and assumed this was a temporary thing caused by stress.

After four years of marriage, Sheila Rudzinski found herself with child. For the second time in Val's life, he found himself the victim of his own selfish lust. He could not be sure, however, that the expected child was his; but what if it were? Because neither wanted to leave their current spouses, they sadly decided to not see each other again, and Sheila's husband would always assume that the expected child was his.

Sheila gave birth to a boy whom they named after Sheila's brother, Davie. Val came by to see the new infant on the pretext of bringing a baby gift to his favorite clients in the new subdivision. After all, he was often in the neighborhood with other new owners. The boy looked just like his older brother, Jeffrey. Val almost cried on the spot, and could not make eye contact with Sheila. He knew he could no longer live in this town knowing another man was raising his child.

Val's excuse to Joyce was that he was bored with the construction business and no longer found it challenging. He was burned out from the long hours away from her and Jeffrey, and longed to get back to the land. After discussing this with Joyce's father, he learned that one of her dad's relatives had a large berry farm for sale near the town of Port Angeles, across the sound on the outskirts of the Olympic National forest. He and Joyce visited the property together. The farmhouse was old, but Val, after having spent those years in construction, told her of all the plans he envisioned for it, giving it every modern convenience. There was a beautiful lake in the backyard which reflected the resplendent mountains in the distance. Joyce, of course, did not want to move farther away from her family, but couldn't help but capture her husband's enthusiasm for the hew enterprise. He had no problem selling his share of the construction business to his partners. Farming was in his blood.

Needless to say, farming oats and hay on a dairy farm in Wisconsin is a bit different than growing strawberries and raspberries in the Pacific Northwest; different soil, different seasonal changes and temperatures. No machines to harvest crops. Berries had to be picked mostly by hand, and within a short window of time. They were a much more delicate crop in all respects. Val had much to learn, and felt he really could use some help. He still had some savings left after selling his part of the construction business and his former home, so he wrote to his brother, Chip in Chicago, and made him a handsome offer. Fifty percent of the business, a full partnership, for his help and expertise. Val knew that Chip's experience with machinery would be an invaluable asset, not to mention, he understood and loved the land as Val did, and he trusted him with his life. If he could just get him out here, Val was certain he'd fall in love with the state just as he did over a dozen years ago.

In Chicago, Chip and Norb were doing well at the filling station and auto repair shop they owned. The first years after the War were a bit lean, but as young families became established, their need for well-maintained transportation and fuel increased. A little pocket money allowed the boys to go out more to bars, dances and movies. It was at one of the neighborhood hangouts, that Chip met Stella, the sassy new waitress and oftentimes barmaid. She was anything but shy, and anyone who frequented the place knew Stella had set her cap for the handsome Chip. Stella was the type of gal that took no grief from anyone, and could put a drunk in his place with a tirade that could make a sailor blush. Everyone at the bar loved her somewhat raucous humor. Stella was the life of the party, and could put down drinks with the best of them. The other regular fellas at the bar teased him unmercifully about the obvious special treatment he received from the cute and sassy Stella, until finally he asked her out to the movies to quiet them, if nothing else.

Chip found her quite different when they were alone together, as if she relaxed and could stop putting on a show for attention. They actually had similar backgrounds, Polish-Catholic offspring of immigrants. Stella was city born and bred, however, and it was obvious from her conversation and tone that she had *been around.* The youngest, and only girl of three siblings, she grew up in a houseful of men. Her mother had died when she was fifteen. Chip would later learn that she had mental problems similar to those of his father, Jan, and had ended her own life. One date led to another, and after learning more about her early years, and meeting her father and brothers, he realized why Stella acted the way she did around men. Her mother was mentally unstable for a good portion of Stella's life, and she was anything but a role model for motherhood or domesticity.

Chip seemed to bring out the best in Stella with his kind demeanor and gentlemanly ways. He treated her like a princess, bringing her small gifts or flowers, and taking her to nice places, almost trying to *make up* for her rough upbringing.

They were married less than a year later. His sisters were surprised by his choice, as she did not seem like Chip's *type,* but you couldn't help but like the girl, she was the life of the party. His mother and siblings were also glad that Chip had finally found someone to build a life with, beginning to think of him as a confirmed bachelor.

Val's letter arrived shortly after Chip and Stella's third anniversary.

They had rented a small duplex near the garage. Their first daughter, they named after Chip's mother, Emily. Stella was pregnant with their second. Val's offer was so out-of-the-blue, that the couple were dumbfounded. It certainly was a generous offer, and a chance to escape the city and return to the land. Stella had never been out of the state except for the occasional road trip north to Wisconsin's lakes in the summer.

Bernice volunteered to watch little Emily, and Norb agreed to hold down the fort at the garage, so Stella and Chip could take the long train trip west. This was terrifically exciting to Stella. She was far enough along in her pregnancy that she was not sickened by the motion of the train, but rather fascinated by the changing landscape as they made their way along. Chip paid extra for sleeping compartments, and they had meals in the dining car. This was a real adventure, and the honeymoon they never had. Chip, too, had been so focused on his business, that he forgot what it meant to have a vacation.

Val met them in Seattle, so he could help them navigate the series of busses and ferries that would take them to the farm. They were awestruck by the majesty of the mountains surrounding them, not to mention, the proximity of the Pacific Ocean.

The farm proved to be nothing like Chip expected. The vast green fields beneath the shadow of the Cascades. It was overwhelming. Val's home was spacious, and had every modern convenience. There was another smaller cabin on the property that would be Chip's. He was assured it, too, would be modernized if they choose to accept Val's offer.

Over the days that followed, Val showed his brother the workings of the farm. Most of their crops were sold to local frozen food companies, or commercial makers of jams and jellies. They also had a field of fragrant mint which grew like weeds here, and because they were Zalewski's, a huge personal vegetable garden and small apple orchard. It was an immense undertaking, and Chip could see why his brother needed the help, and also, the huge potential in the enterprise.

In addition to the idea of taking a huge step into the unknown and leaving the business in Chicago he had worked so hard to build up, there was the problem with Joyce and Stella's relationship. They could not be more different. Joyce was very lady-like and reserved, much like a model for an appliance commercial. She talked about raising her two boys, gardening, and where to shop for fashions in town. Stella would rather have drinks and cigarettes with the brothers. Would this work?

On the long train ride back to Chicago, they decided that after the new baby was born, they would take Val up on his offer, and move west in time for the next harvest. In the meantime, Val would update Chip on the day-to-day business of running the farm via post.

Norb had recently begun dating the daughter of one of his mother's neighborhood friends. In fact, the two had actually gone to the same high school, but Norb was four years older. The two matchmakers were, indeed, successful. The young people were head-over-heels for each other. Chip had recently approached Norb with the idea of buying out his share of the business. Perhaps an obvious omen, his fiancé Adele's father had just offered to take Norb on at his business, as he had no sons of his own to apprentice. The garage was sold at a healthy profit for them both. Chip Zalewski headed to the Pacific Northwest find his future, and Norb Glowacki to the newly expanding suburbs of Chicago.

Norb and Adele's wedding was a lovely affair, her father sparing no expense for his only child. The two mothers were beaming in their new dresses and hats, purchased from the sale rack at Marshall-Fields department store downtown, and enhanced by large white orchid corsages. The entire Zalewski clan gathered in Chicago to celebrate, minus Val and Joyce. Even the two nuns were allowed to come. It was the first time they had all been together since Jan's funeral. This was only the second time Ben and Chip had seen each other since Chip left 𝕿𝖍𝖊 𝕽𝖊𝖉 𝖅 at fifteen.

Emilia was thrilled to see the first of her grandchildren marry. Gladys had taken her shopping in Milwaukee for a new store bought outfit for the occasion. She remarked that it was one of the best days of her life, seeing all her family gathered for such a joyous occasion.

Chip and recently engaged Henry Milewski were in the wedding party. Wendy's three year old daughter, Diane, was the flower girl, walking daintily just before the bride, processing up the long church aisle to the altar, throwing rose petals from her little basket as she had practiced the evening before. What was not at the rehearsal however, was the music, and when the organist broke into the loud and dramatic introduction to the Wedding March, the frightened little girl screamed and went running to her mother standing at the back of the church! Of course, the rest of the congregation thought it splendidly adorable.

Chip and Ben's reunion was awkward to say the least, the older being too stubborn to apologize, and the wound being too deep for the younger to heal anyway. Clumsy introductions were made to each other's spouses and children, and after that, they avoided one another for the rest of the evening. Neither Stella nor Irene ever knew the entire story of the falling-out between the brothers, and both knew better than to press for details. *Sr. Phil* ever the peacemaker, did her best to try to reconcile the two through her prayers and letters to each after Chip left, but to no avail. Some breaks did not mend.

THE SIXTIES

By 1960, Emilia was approaching eighty. Although in relatively good health, it was getting difficult for her to climb the steep narrow staircase leading to the flat she shared with Mary Grych in Stevens Crossing for over ten years. Mary, too, had her aches and pains, and the house and garden were beginning to be burdensome. It was decided that Emilia should move in with Gladys.

Al's alcoholism never dissipated. The situation came to a head when Al suffered a severe health crisis which landed him in the hospital for several weeks. The diagnosis was Chlorosis of the liver. Gladys was told he had a less than fifty per cent chance of recovery. The priest was called in to give last rights, and his little niece, Diane, was cautiously sneaked in to say *goodbye*, as rules did not allow anyone under sixteen to visit. Miraculously, Al recovered after enduring not only his disease, but the painful process of withdrawal. Doctors warned him that if he continued to drink, he would probably not survive.

The cure did not last, and after four months sober, Al went on a week-long bender. Gladys, ever the good Catholic, again sought the guidance of her confessor. As divorce was not approved by the Church, it was out of the question in her mind, but because Al's behavior was so reprehensible when he had been drinking, the priest suggested for her health and sanity that they separate. Al took cheap lodging in an upper flat duplex near the factory where he was somehow still employed, the quintessential mark of a functioning alcoholic. He begged Gladys not to make him leave, but after many difficult conversations with their parish priest, he acquiesced.

So Emilia began the fourth and final stage of her life, now moving all her earthly belongings into the extra bedroom at Gladys' home in Milwaukee. Fritz and Wendy lived near, so she had family around weekends to share meals and games of pinochle with. Unfortunately, Gladys needed a full time job, as Al spent much of his meager paycheck at the corner tavern and on sustenance for his small flat. This meant she was unable to take her mother to daily Mass, which Emilia had become so accustomed to doing with Mary. Gladys' church was not in a Polish neighborhood as was hers in Stevens Crossing, and because she had refused to speak English for so long, she had little communication not only with her priest there, but with the other parishioners as well.

She spent her days keeping the house up for Gladys, doing some of the cooking and baking, and praying in front of her beloved Madonna, for whom she had created a special niche in her room. Unfortunately, her arthritic fingers no longer allowed her to do a lot of the crafting and needlework she once enjoyed, but she was limber enough to teach her grandchildren who visited how to decorate Easter eggs with beeswax, do simple embroidery stitches on pillowcases and flour sack towels, or to tie chruscki donut knots.

She lived for letters from home, especially those from Irene, still at 𝕿𝖍𝖊 𝕽𝖊𝖉 𝖅. Irene wrote long, newsy letters filled with local goings-on and the latest gossip. Telephone lines had recently been run to the farm, so they now had their own telephone, not a private line mind you, but it meant no more running to Chula's to make or take a call. At this time, any phone calls over a few mile radius were considered *long-distance,* and the charge for these calls, timed by the minute, seemed exorbitant, so calls to those outside Stevens Crossing were rare. Such progress. Gladys also had a television set and a hi-fidelity record player, both of which Emilia thought extravagant. She admittedly loved the television however, especially the musical shows like *Liberace* or *Lawrence Welk*, who both being of Polish descent, often played a lively polka or two, and required no translation.

By now, Val and Chip's business was doing extremely well. Val had two boys, and Chip two girls and a boy. Stella and Joyce were anything but close, but the two couples did spend time together playing cards or sharing a meal. When the men retired to the porch for rye and smokes, Stella was right there with them, drink-for-drink, while Joyce stayed in with a movie magazine or the TV.

Joyce wondered how Stella could function as a wife and mother after a night of drinking with the men. She often heard her at the school bus stop. It seemed Stella never talked to her children, rather she shrieked at them, almost like a sergeant shouting orders to his recruits, complete with expletives. Was this the product of her hangovers or just her personality, she wondered. Joyce worried for the children, but knew Chip as kind and warm-hearted, and perhaps this compensated for their seemingly cold-hearted mother.

Stella, on the other hand, wondered how a woman could be so blind. It was obvious to everyone else on the farm, that Val had been having an affair with Sheila, the young widow from a neighboring farm. It seems this woman used every excuse to visit, asking Val to help repair this or that, or for advice on hiring pickers or perhaps on selling the farm. Val seemed to spend more and more time in town, running this errand or that. Joyce didn't drive, so it did not seem unusual for him to do this. He also spent several evenings a week at a local tavern. His wife knew he had a love affair with rye whiskey, but it never entered her mind that he would also have an affair with another woman.

When Stella confronted Chip about her suspicions, he adamantly denied it, although he knew she was right. He had seen them together at the tavern, hands all over each other. Chip was worried someone would tell Joyce, as gossip spread quickly, and the couple seemed to be unconcerned about their public display of affection. Perhaps it was deliberate; perhaps the grieving widow wanted Val to leave his wife and hoped he would be put in the position to do so. In any event, Chip did not want to see his brother's marriage implode, so when an opportune time arose sipping whiskey after a long day of cultivating, he casually mentioned that there was talk about town that he and Sheila were an item. Val laughed it off, admitting that Sheila was quite a looker, and he wouldn't mind taking her to bed, but not to listen to drunken gossip. Then Chip told him how he'd seen them kissing when he unexpectedly wandered into the equipment shed two weeks prior. Val then made a somewhat crude comment about "adding some excitement to the old married life", and how he shouldn't "knock it 'til he tried it." "After all", he retorted, "you can't be getting much from that drunk you married." Chip somehow resisted his first inclination which was to knock his brother's head off, and instead abruptly got up and left, one large tear running down his cheek.

Not surprising, it was Stella who informed Joyce of her husband's infidelity. Her children had been spending more and more time with Joyce after school in the winter months, Stella complaining that she needed quiet and bed rest for her headaches. In the warmer months the children, looking somewhat like poor orphans, were shooed outside, so mommy could rest. Joyce attributed it to hangovers. When she tried to confront Stella about the children being dirty, spoiled and unsupervised, Stella snapped. She had always felt insecure next to her sister-in-law, who was brought up as the only child of a successful farmer and his wife, whereas she, a city kid from an immigrant neighborhood in Chicago, raised as the only girl with three big brothers to care for as her mentally unstable mother died when she was young. Her physical pain and mental anguish of not being able to physically care for her children spewed out. "At least my husband is faithful to me!", Stella blurted. The tirade continued until Joyce ran from her sobbing.

Val and Joyce suffered a messy and painful divorce. Sheila did not "get her man", and Stella died of a brain tumor a few years later.

The religious niece and aunt were finally reunited, when Sr. Ernest Marie was reassigned to a parochial school in Chicago, first as a teacher, and later, principal. Josie was overjoyed to have her daughter close again. Her husband, Joe, had not survived a massive heart attack, shortly after his retirement, thus Josie's depression worsened. She also began to have minor seizures, finally diagnosed as epilepsy. Henry and Sr. Ernest, concerned with her well-being, sold the modest family home in the city, and purchased a newer duplex in the suburbs where Josie could occupy the bottom floor. Henry, his wife and three small children would live above. Their new residence was near the nuns' motherhouse, which made visits more convenient. Josie was close to seventy and had survived the death of her mother, immigration to a foreign land, up-bringing by a step-mother, grueling farm duties, the responsibilities of caring for her younger siblings, two World Wars, the Great Depression, the death of her firstborn son, and a tragic fire that all but destroyed her and her beloved, Joe.

Lawrence and Gene had three sons and two daughters, and lived less than a mile from the school where he would complete his entire teaching career. He never lost his passion for fishing, and passed this on to his sons. They never missed an opportunity to take their small boat out on one of the many Wisconsin lakes in the area. Their home, although not overly large on the main floor, had space for many bedrooms upstairs, and, in the summer, room for sleeping on the screened front and large back porches. It was here that the Milwaukee relatives spent many a summer vacation.

The ladies usually spent the days watching the kids swim in one of the favorite nearby lakes, picking seasonal favorites in the garden, or a car trip to nearby Stevens Crossing to peruse the shops and stop for a thick, cold malted milk shake at the town dairy. The cousins would reminisce in later years about the anticipation and delight of these treats, and how they never had a whole one to themselves, but always had to split them a few ways.

The city cousins were always enamored with all small town rural life had to offer. They could walk the two blocks "downtown" or to the park, catch pollywogs or fish in the creek across the street, or go for a swim in the lake. Often they would go on treasure hunts around the small town looking for glass bottles that they could then sell back for a penny each at the grocery market. These coins were quickly returned to the grocer in exchange for red licorice whips, root beer bottle caps, candy cigarettes or some other "penny candy". After dinner, the uncles would walk down to the neighborhood tap. Stories are recounted that the cousins would follow the men into the bar. The men, not wanting to be bothered or tattled-on to their wives, would bribe the kids with loose change to go away. It was especially profitable when Uncle Jack or Uncle Al were in town!

Al, Bob and Fritz all loved fishing the sparkling clear central Wisconsin lakes as well. Even Jack Glowacki from Chicago joined them at times. No one enjoyed the mass fish cleaning in the backyard, but cold beer and camaraderie made it easier. The real reward, was the feast the ladies later created with the finished perch, blue gill, crappie and if very lucky, trout. Gene was known for her fish fries, accompanied by fresh cut garden salad with warm bacon dressing, steamy corn on the cob, homemade dill pickles and warm, buttery yeast rolls. They had a huge garden and canned all they needed for colder months. The other ladies in the family would marvel at how Gene could stretch a dollar. After all, what choice did she have raising five children on a teacher's salary?

Depression-Era lessons never faded. In later years, Gene and her sister-in-law Wendy, would form a "couponing club" where they saved box tops, labels, and later *UPC* codes from grocery goods, to send in to manufactures offering refunds and the like. They shopped together when they could to see how many items they could get for "free", especially on *double and triple coupon day* at their local market. Their grown children would often find their own pantries stripped of can labels and box tops after one of their moms had visited. No one complained, however, when refund checks unexpectedly showed up in the mail. Often refunds were only one per family, and the two women, of course not wanting to miss an opportunity to get "free money", used their relatives addresses. It was a fun and lucrative game. When Gene passed away, her family found box upon box of neatly filed box tops, labels and UPC codes. When Wendy passed, her daughter found dozens of tubes of "free" toothpaste and all manner of stockpiled toiletries and grocery items.

Of course no trip to Uncle Lawrence's was complete without a trip to 𝕿𝖍𝖊 𝕽𝖊𝖉 𝖅. Ben and Irene continued to work the farm, although they did sell off several acres when it was profitable for them to do so. Two of their four children had left the farm to marry and begin families of their own, which just left Ben and his younger son and daughter to help with chores. By now electricity had come to 𝕿𝖍𝖊 𝕽𝖊𝖉 𝖅, allowing for time-saving devices like milking machines, but even those took human effort. Delores, Ben's oldest daughter, remembered when electric lights were installed in their farmhouse around 1946, and how she and her brother would fight to see who got to flip the magical switch each evening to turn on the new lamps which Ben had made.

The city cousins were always interested to see Uncle Ben's newest project. He had created a pair of intricately pierced and carved wooden panels that he and his sons installed between the living and dining rooms creating a type of room divider. The remarkable Persian inspired design was original, based on some old sketches he had kept from his visits to the Art Institute in Chicago. Relatives and friends were duly impressed. His newest creation in the 1960's was a twenty- two foot tall totem pole carved and painted from a huge white pine log cut from his property. He placed it near 𝕿𝖍𝖊 𝕽𝖊𝖉 𝖅 sign, at the entrance to the farm. It was a remarkable and imposing structure, sporting many expressive faces, heavily textured feathers and even a spread-wing eagle at the top. Many passing cars would slow to look and admire it.

The Steven's Crossing newspaper even interviewed Ben and took pictures of the totem for a newspaper article. Emilia was so proud when she received the clipping from Irene! No relative visiting the farm ever left without a piece of Irene's famous fruit pie and one of Ben's creations; wooden cookie jars, lamps or one of his "signature" swans, always just signed *Z*.

The 1960's was marked by the Civil Rights Movement and the War in Vietnam with its violent protests, draft lotteries and draft dodgers. There were also several political assassinations, including John F. Kennedy, the first Irish Catholic president, as well as the brilliant voice of Civil Rights, Martin Luther King Jr. The decade also saw the impact of the *British Invasion* on music from groups like the Beatles. The counterculture *beatniks* of the previous decade were replaced by the love pontificating *hippies,* especially on the west coast. By the time the first man walked on the moon in 1969, Ben was closing in on sixty-five, and retirement. They had a decision to make, to keep the farm in the family, or sell it, its soil stained with the blood, sweat and tears of two young immigrants.

The young men in the family, like many of their fathers, were faced with a military draft imposed by then President Johnson in 1965, to supplement the volunteer force fighting in Southeast Asia. Males born between 1944 and 1950 were eligible. Again, there were exemptions.

Ben's two sons were past draft age, Fred already married with a young child of his own. Val's two boys however, were both called up. The older, Jeffrey, had completed medical school, was drafted into the Army as a Captain, and after initial boot camp training, sent to a Medical Evacuation Hospital in Vietnam where he served one grueling year. The younger son, Steven, had decided to remain in the family business with his father. When news of a draft "lottery" was announced, he volunteered, rather than wait for the agony of possibly having his birthdate called each month. He enlisted in the relatively new Air Force, like his father wished he could have done in the previous World War. He would make it his career. Steven did not have to serve in Vietnam however, as two brothers could not both serve in a combat zone at the same time. After eventually completing Officer Training School, he was accepted into flight school.

Lawrence's two older sons each had educational deferments, and the youngest had not yet reached eighteen during the draft years nor did Henry Milewski's sons. Wendy's son came of age toward the end of the Vietnam War era. So the "sons of the sons" survived yet another War.

By the 1970's, Emilia was near ninety. She had survived to see all of her offspring to adulthood, leading prosperous American lives. The children made it possible for her to have comfortable retirement years where she could spend time with her grandchildren, and travel to places like Washington State on an airplane, nonetheless. When Al retired, Gladys took him back into her home where she could keep an eye on him lest he drink himself to death day-in and day out. Because Gladys made him sleep in a separate room, Emilia was sent to live nearby with her youngest daughter, Wendy. Her two children were now out of the house and starting their own lives, so they had the extra room. Wendy was able to take her to daily Mass and the now more frequent doctor's appointments. Fritz and Jean were regular visitors, and Bob was a willing driver for trips to Steven's Crossing or Chicago, where Sr. Philothea always managed to procure him a cold beer or two for his efforts in chauffeuring.

THE SEVENTIES

On January 1st, 1972, Irene awoke early to feed the chickens and gather eggs before getting ready for Mass. The first day of the New Year was typical for Wisconsin, frosty cold, but bright sunshine making the mounds of fresh snow sparkle in the morning light. She and Ben had spent a quiet New Year's Eve, watching Lawrence Welk conduct his orchestra on television, the cast of entertainers singing standards of yesteryear and of course *Auld Lang Singe*. They both adored the show. Ben especially enjoyed seeing the lovely sets and beautiful costumes worn by the famous cast members. He always had to keep up with the latest trends, even if he, himself, could not always afford to. Before they retired that evening, he and Irene reminisced on the past year and recent holiday events. The two boys and their families had joined them for Christmas Eve and Christmas Day. Their oldest daughter, Delores, her two children, and her husband now lived in New Jersey where he had a medical practice. They were unable to join Ben and Irene for the holidays as he was "on call", at the hospital. Their youngest girl, Sally, was a newlywed. She and her Air Force husband were stationed in San Antonio, Texas, and could not get leave. Although they missed having their entire brood around the holiday table, it was great to have the boys and the grandchildren, especially Fred, as he now lived in Milwaukee. A *car guy* like his godfather Fritz, Fred worked for a major auto manufacturer, and raced stock cars as a hobby. Like all of his Uncles, he was also an avid sportsman, especially hunting and fishing. Ben framed the picture Fred's wife sent him, cut from *Wisconsin Waters* magazine, showing his son holding a prize winning bass.

The retired farmer and his wife thought back on the previous year when the difficult decision was made to stop planting, sell the livestock, machinery and some of the land. More and more small farms were being purchased by large agricultural corporations. The future of farming as Ben knew it, was unknown. The remaining property would be divided among his four children. His son, Ken, had mentioned an interest in the house, should Ben decide to sell it. Emilia had deeded it to him years before, as none of the other siblings expressed interest.

A grand celebration had been held in June when their youngest daughter wed. Perhaps because it was his last child to marry, Ben insisted on an impressive affair. Sally was marrying the son of one of the more successful potato farmers in the area. It would be a large festivity, with much of the surrounding community in attendance. Ben even insisted on going with his wife and daughter to pick out the wedding gown and mother-of-the-bride dress in Wausau insisting on the latest fashion.

The entire Zalewski clan attended, even the Washington brothers and the two nuns. Emilia was now in her late eighties, and the family knew this was an opportunity for them to see their mother while she was still in fairly good health, an occasion for one last family picture. Three of this smiling group would pass by year's end.

Wendy and Bob were in great spirits this holiday season. Their daughter became engaged to her high school sweetheart, which was cause for celebration. They had all been invited to an engagement brunch that New Year's Day given by one of Bob's best friends and work associates. Wendy could not help but notice Bob's quiet demeanor on the ride there. Perhaps he was a bit hungover from the New Year's Eve festivities the night before. When she watched him consume several Bloody Mary's before brunch, she began to worry. Shortly after brunch, she noticed her husband nursing another Miller High Life, conversing with his friend in whispered tones, while the women were deep in wedding talk. Usually the life of the party, he seemed eager to leave. His Green Bay Packers were not playing until six, and it was barely two. After thanks, *Happy New Year's*, and goodbyes, their daughter's fiancée offered to chauffeur them home, as it was clear Bob was not in shape to drive. It was then that Bob told them of his early phone call from Stevens Crossing. Ben had died in his sleep of what appeared to be a massive stroke. Not wanting to spoil the day for his daughter, and see the grief it would bring to his wife, not to mention his mother-in-law, he had held out as long as he could.

They had dropped Emilia off at Gladys' house, where Fritz and Jean had driven over for a New Year's Day feast of pork roast and sauerkraut, potato and mushroom pierogi, blackberry brandy, decadent sweets, and of course, several rousing games of Emilia's favorite pinochle. No wonder Bob had gotten the call instead of Fritz. He must have driven to Gladys' right after Mass. It was all Bob could do to walk through her door. Emilia had survived her first-born son. It was not natural, but she accepted it as she did all things, as God's plan.

And so the clan gathered again at 𝕿𝖍𝖊 𝕽𝖊𝖉 𝖅, the second time in just six months, not in celebration, but in mourning. The day of the funeral was frigidly cold, but thankfully no early January snow storms came to heed the bereaved as they travelled from Chicago, Milwaukee and the west coast. The siblings were of course concerned for Ben's widow Irene, but she had one son and his family nearby, as well as her own siblings. Her mother Mary was ailing, but still managed to come to the funeral to pay her respects to her dear friend and old housemate, Emilia. She was a great comfort to Emilia, as they were able to reminisce, and speak in their native tongue. Ben's daughters persuaded old Fr. Sulek to come out of retirement in Wausau, to say Ben's funeral Mass. This familiarity was also comforting for Emilia and all the siblings. The girls planned a grand affair, as they knew so well what their father liked. It was a High Mass with full choir and all Ben's favorite hymns. The entire community knew how much Ben loved flowers, and the bouquets were exquisite, even in January. Afterward, Ben's oldest daughter and her husband invited everyone to a reception at the Polish Hall, the scene of so many happy gatherings in the past. Old neighbors and friends brought platters of food and bottles of blackberry brandy. His oldest son, Fred eulogized his father, recalling his early struggles being an immigrant child in a foreign land, having to absorb a new language, learn to build, plant and care for livestock. He lived through two World Wars, Korea and Vietnam not to mention, the Great Depression. He was a survivor, who by his sacrifices, improved life for his children and grandchildren. Fred also spoke of his stubbornness, and often tough demeanor, tempered by his passion for beauty whether it be in the form of his lovely wife and family, music, movies, gardens, fashion, travel or art. Just this past autumn, Ben had been asked by the gallery curator at the State College in Stevens Crossing, to exhibit pieces of his woodcarvings. His totem pole carving at 𝕿𝖍𝖊 𝕽𝖊𝖉 𝖅 had gained him a reputation. He was reluctant at first, as he did not feel he was intellectually suited for such an experience, but Irene and the children talked him into it, and it was praised by many; to his surprise and delight, he even sold a few pieces.

Chip's gentle nature and a few shots of brandy got the best of him, forcing him to leave the hall mid-tribute, lest his sobs be heard by all. A lifetime of emotions surfaced, as he recalled how his teenage encounter with his now deceased oldest brother, the bicycle and an ax, changed the course of his life forever. It still hurt after thirty five years.

Also attending the funeral was Annie Pacwa, formerly Annie Chula, Val's first crush from the nearby tavern where they used to make calls and receive their phone messages. He would recognize that smile anywhere. During a conversation with her and his sisters, he learned that she was widowed a year ago, and had sold the family home and moved to an apartment in Stevens Crossing where she had a small dress shop. Of course she invited the girls to come see the shop if they had time before heading back after the funeral. Her flirtation with Val was obvious to Wendy and Gladys, and they teased him mercilessly back at 𝕿𝖍𝖊 𝕽𝖊𝖉 𝖅. Unlike his sisters who were staying with Lawrence and Gene, Val had taken a room in town. He stayed two weeks on the pretense of helping Irene settle things, but in reality, making his boyhood fantasies a reality. They were two consenting adults after all, and it was *the 70's* . Unfortunately, Irene still had to live with the small town gossip long after Val went back to Washington.

Josie had not made the trip to Wisconsin for the funeral. Although she was still living with Henry and his wife, her dementia progressed, and she also developed severe seizures. Because of this, they were forced to put her into a nursing facility. Henry and Lorrie now had four children, and she was pregnant with their fifth. Although it broke their hearts, it was an impossible task to care for someone so ill, and five children, too. Bernice visited as often as she could, as did the nuns. She had not even been told of Ben's death, as the doctor's did not believe she could comprehend it. She cried a lot, and kept repeating, "Georgie". The long-suffering Josie slipped away after having suffered a severe seizure in early May, now reunited with her beloved Joe and Georgie. Emilia lost another child. Even though Josie was her step-daughter, she always thought of her as her own. They had in a way, grown up together, bonded by their love of Jan, and their early émigré struggles.

Needless to say, these losses took a toll on Emilia whose age and physical condition were already causing her to decline. She still attended daily Mass when she felt up to it, and fair weather prevailed.

Miraculously, a priest of Polish descent was assigned to Gladys and Wendy's parish. Fr. Warzianiakowski (or Fr. Joe as his congregants called him) did not say Mass in Polish, but was able to converse with Emilia and hear her confession.

A body strengthened by hard work in her youth, still served her in her old age. Although slower, she could still get around without a cane or walker. Incredibly, she did not often get colds and flu, and had never been a patient in a hospital. Her hair was gray, but still thick. The long braids and buns her youth were replaced by stylish dos kept short and permed by her nearby granddaughter, a professional hair stylist. Her pierced ears which at one time were the condescending mark of an immigrant, were now in vogue as her younger granddaughters were quick to point out. The work-worn hands were still able to knead bread and fill pierogi.

Travel was now restricted to the occasional weekend visit to see Fritz and Jean for poker or bunko games, or if she were up to it, a drive to Chicago to see Bernice and the nuns. The almost four hour car trip to Stevens Crossing was just too tiring. Her room was filled with various religious images, especially prominent being the picture of the Black Madonna, her protector, brought from her homeland, and the statue from Jan given to her for their first Christmas in America, and another carved by her son Ben. The grandchildren contributed to her shrines with gifts of votive candles, holy cards and the like, each treasure displayed and cherished.

Wendy's daughter, Diane, was living at an Air Force base in west Texas with her pilot husband, when she received the long distance call from her mother. Busia Emily had developed an unusual cough, and after nearly a week, and amid Emilia's protestations, a doctor was called to the house. After listening to her lungs, the doctor called for an ambulance. It would be Emilia's first and last time in a hospital. Despite rounds of fluids and antibiotics, she was not getting better. Fr. Joe was called in for Last Rights. Minutes later with her tearful daughters around her, she left her earthly home to join her beloved Jan, Ben and Josie.

Unfortunately, Fr. Sulek, their old parish priest, had died shortly after having said Ben's funeral Mass. The new curate of St. Casmir's, also of Polish descent, conducted the services. It gave the surviving family members great joy to see how many attended the service and wake the evening before. She was beloved and remembered fondly by the community, even after having left years ago. There were still a few elders who shared stories of Emilia's piety, talents and generosity, especially during the Depression.

Many remarked on how well she was able to cope with Jan and his illness in his later years. She rarely complained or thought of herself. Even after having learned the dreadful fate of her parents and siblings at the hands of the Nazis during World War II, she continued to send small amounts of money she secretly saved, along with boxes of outgrown clothing, and hand knit items to her surviving relatives in Sulwaki, now under Communist rule.

She was buried in the church graveyard beside Jan, and adjacent to the headstones of her dear departed Stan and Genja. Ben was laid to rest in the same vicinity. So many with Polish surnames; if each could speak of their lives, what stories they could tell of heroes and villains: what history would be revealed.

Emilia Ulewicz Zalewski survived seventeen American presidents, and eight Popes. How thrilled she would have been to see the next Pope come from her own home country!

This young, innocent, incredibly strong Polish girl, immigrated to a foreign country under less-than-ideal circumstances, where she did not even know the language, and built a home, farm, and life for her husband and family, from nothing. She raised her widowed husband's young daughter as her own, endured the home births of eleven children, and the heart-wrenching deaths of two infants. She buried two of her adult children, as well. Emilia's life bridged four major wars, from which she diligently prayed her sons and grandsons would safely return. The Nazis and later the Russians exterminated most of her remaining family in war-ravaged Poland. Not knowing their fate for years on end, brought no end of torment. The misery brought on by the Great Depression was all but indescribable, on an already struggling immigrant family, and in many ways, divided her nearest and dearest forever.

During Emilia's lifetime she would also experience modern marvels, such as automobiles, jet airplanes, electricity, motion pictures, radio and television. Work-saving combines, milking machines, automatic washers and dryers would be produced. She would witness the first man walking on the moon, and the assassination of an American president. Pandemics such as Spanish flu and polio were both feared and conquered. Doctors would prolong life with artificial hearts and organ transplants.

Lawrence would be the last of Emilia's children to pass at 92 years of age. Jan and Emilia would produce 15 grandchildren, and Emilia would live to see the birth of fifteen great-grandchildren. Among them and their off-spring would be next-generation farmers, teachers, doctors, dentists, veterinarians, scientists, race car drivers, gardening enthusiasts, writers, engineers, cooks and bakers, horse-breeders, flight attendants, beauticians, military officers and veterans, business owners, hunters and fishermen, entrepreneurs, computer wizards, needle workers, artists and craftsmen, readers and book-lovers, musicians, members of religious communities, devoted lay church ministers, and loving mothers and fathers. A proud legacy, marked by 𝕮𝖍𝖊 𝕽𝖊𝖉 𝖅.

EPILOGUE

And so, after twenty years, in my retirement, I have finally found time to put pen to paper (or fingertips to keyboard!) What would Jan and Emilia think of computers? If my great-grandchildren are reading this, they are probably wondering how I worked on such an antiquated thing as a PC.

It is 5 AM, on a cold Midwestern March day, and I am grumbling about how long the heater has taken to kick in. I really want coffee, but am out of milk. I'll have to drive one block to the local mini-mart later and pick some up. Meanwhile, I'll have a cup of tea. The two minutes I have to wait for the microwave to heat the water is annoying. I turn on the TV and they are talking about Americans growing aggravation with the rising price of fuel and food. And, there is talk of World War. The more things change, the more they stay the same.

I cannot even fathom my grandparent's day-to-day reality. Their physical and mental strength puts me to shame. It is hard to wrap my head around this sometimes, living as I do in the twenty-first century. I owe my very existence to them.

I never knew my grandfather, as he died before I was born. I knew my Busia, however. She even lived with us for a while. I remember her trying to teach me Polish. As a kid I thought this foreign language speaking *un-cool*, and was less-than-interested; perhaps even embarrassed. The mistakes of youth. Sorry Busia! Thanks for teaching me how to make pysanky Easter eggs. I still make them every year. A few years ago, I had a chruscki making party with my two daughters and my daughter-in-law, via *zoom*, each in our own kitchens. We vied to see who could make the prettiest one...I did not win! You would have loved it.

I feel your presence at times. My daughter wanted to wear her grandmother's veil on her wedding day. The dress you so beautifully crafted out of Uncle Chip's parachute silk had begun to disintegrate a bit, and the veil, itself had a few holes, but I managed to save all the lace edging, and attach it to some fresh tulle, using the old as a pattern. As I hand-sewed at my dining room table, I could feel you, mother, and the aunts there with me. It was the oddest yet glorious feeling.

Sometimes I feel sorry for my own children not having the huge family of aunts, uncles and cousins that I had. Each aunt was *another mother* to me. My cousins were my best friends. Sadly, the aunts and uncles have now all passed, and I regret not milking them for every scrap of history I could. I hope future generations will never forget the sacrifices of their ancestors, for they were many.

As I am finishing this epistle, the clock radio in my husband's office is playing static-y music. My husband is still asleep and that radio hasn't worked in over twenty years. Busia, ja cie kochem.

ACKNOWLEDGEMENTS

This book is a work of fiction. Although much of it is based on stories and traditions passed down through the generations, the stories and characters in many cases have been changed and/or embellished. It is not meant to be an actual historical record of people and events.

Thank you to my main editors, Elaine Plummer and my husband and best friend, John Mitchel.

Thanks be to God who gave me this time to share my thoughts with future generations, lest past sacrifices be forgotten in time.

Finally, thanks to my dear Uncle Chip for sharing many of these stories with me.

Cover design: Ashley E. Day and Diane M. Mitchel, 2022